Harvey K. Hines

At Sea and in Port

Or, life and experience of William S. Fletcher, for thirty years seaman's missionary

in Portland, Oregon

Harvey K. Hines

At Sea and in Port
Or, life and experience of William S. Fletcher, for thirty years seaman's missionary in Portland, Oregon

ISBN/EAN: 9783337093914

Printed in Europe, USA, Canada, Australia, Japan

Cover: Foto ©Raphael Reischuk / pixelio.de

More available books at **www.hansebooks.com**

William S. Fletcher,
The Seaman's Missionary.

AT SEA AND IN PORT

OR

LIFE AND EXPERIENCE

OF

WILLIAM S. FLETCHER

FOR THIRTY YEARS SEAMAN'S MISSIONARY
IN PORTLAND, OREGON.

Compiled from his Journal and other authentic sources

BY

H. K. HINES, D. D.

With an introduction

BY

BISHOP EARL CRANSTON.

———

PRICE, $1.00.

———

THE J. K. GILL COMPANY,
Portland, Oregon.
——
1898.

Press of Marsh Printing Company, Portland.

Dedication.

To my brethren of the Sea, in whose labors and sorrows I have
shared, and in whose happiness I have rejoiced
from my boyhood, this record of my life
and experience is most
affectionately

Dedicated

in the steadfast hope that it will prove to them a beacon and
a guide to the Port of Endless Peace.

WILLIAM S. FLETCHER.

CONTENTS.

—

INTRODUCTION.

✿ ✿ ✿

IT will be well for those who propose to read this unpretentious volume to understand at once its mission. It is not sent forth as the life-story of a man who fancies that he has won a high place amongst men. Nor is Br. Fletcher covetous of literary recognition or of the rewards that ordinarily attend successful authorship. He is only a plain Christian man, who, in what he has to communicate, seeks to honor his Master rather than himself. As the representative of the Seaman's Friend Society in this city, Mr. Fletcher has been not only an enthusiastic witness for Christ in all assemblies, but a tireless missionary among the sailors visiting this port. I am sure that in thus introducing him I can express no desire more in accord with his own design and purpose than that the story of his rescue shall be to many a sin-

wrecked sailor a life-line thrown by the hand of a
saved shipmate.

Surely other lives than those of "great men"
should "remind us (that) we may make our lives
sublime; and, departing, leave behind us"—ay,
something better than—"footprints on the sands
of time." After all, greatness consists first in
character. It is Divine possession, only, that
makes man capable of deeds worth telling—deeds
that do not pale in the presence of the motive that
prompted them. We have heard of savages who
were prodigies in cunning and courage, but mon-
strosities as men. Beasts of prey can leave footprints in the sand. "Greatness," as measured in
the past, often stalked with bloody trail over the
rights and liberties of man. But we have learned,
and the world is fast learning the truer type. "The
Light that lighteth every man" has not been shining in vain. The greatest life ever lived was that
of Jesus the Christ. From pole to pole, and the
earth around, He is crowned the Ideal Man, and
the Saviour of men. Think of it : that two
should be one. The result of this accepted truth
upon the world's measurements of men is being
wrought out slowly, but the revolution is on and

will prove resistless. Henceforth the true man, the brave man, the perfect man,—the great man, if you will,—is to be the friend and saviour of men; not an oppressor, not a plunderer of his kind. So let it be. Good-bye to the stars that rose in selfish ambition, lust and carnage. Welcome the new galaxy with Christ as its central sun, and this its prophetic legend:

"THEY THAT TURN MANY TO RIGHTEOUSNESS SHALL SHINE AS THE STARS FOREVER AND EVER."—[Daniel xii: 3.]

No; the author of "At Sea and in Port," is not seeking reputation. But if God shall bless his witness to the men "who go down to the sea in ships," many may yet come from all nations and call him great, because honored of his Lord. Amen.

EARL CRANSTON.

Portland, Oregon, March 20, 1898.

PRELUDE.

♣ ♣ ♣

AS Compiler and Editor of this Memoir of Mr. William S. Fletcher, it is suitable that I should say that those portions of this book appearing as my own are the result of an intimate personal acquaintance with Mr. Fletcher and his work that has continued for over thirty years. They express the personal estimate that so long and so intimate a knowledge of the man and his work has enabled me to form of them. Pure and incorruptible, devout and consecrated, firm, yet kind and charitable, his life has been a beacon to voyagers over the ocean, and a guide to toilers on the land.

H. K. HINES.

Portland, Oregon, April, 1898.

CHAPTER I.

BIRTH AND EARLY LIFE.

"I am: How little more I know!
Whence came I? Whither do I go?
A centered self, which feels and is;
A cry between the silences;
A shadow birth of clouds at strife
With sunshine on the hills of life;
A shaft from Nature's quiver cast
Into the Future from the Past!
Between the cradle and the shroud.
A meteors' flight from cloud to cloud."

—Whittier.

WILLIAM S. FLETCHER was the oldest child of William Fletcher, and was born in the parish of Kilmore, near the town of Neaugh, County Tipperary, Ireland, on the 29th day of May, 1829. His parents were members of the Roman Catholic Church, and the boy was brought up in its faith. When he was seven years of age his father died, and soon after his mother married again. The next seven years he spent at home, but at fourteen he left his home, or, as he says, "ran away from home," and soon reached the port of Limerick, with the intention of going to sea. He had but a few pennies in his pocket, but, as he had come with the intention of going to sea, he soon found his way to the deck of a ship and asked the captain if he would take him "and make a sailor of him." The captain took him and William remained with him for more than two years in the Quebec trade. He finally left this ship in Quebec and worked his way to New York, and after spending a couple of weeks in that great city shipped on one of the "Black Ball" line for Liverpool. On the return of the vessel to New York it brought over six hundred emigrants.

For some years there was nothing in the life of this young man unlike that which enters into the life of any young seaman. He made a number of voyages out of New York to various European ports, and also to South America. In one of his European voyages he brought out a younger brother with him and apprenticed him to the sail-maker's trade in a large Sail and Rigging Loft in South Street, in New York. On another voyage to Dublin he brought his sister with him on his return. He had found an aunt in his ramblings about the city of New York, on another occasion, and he left his sister with her, and himself entered a sailor boarding house kept by one Sam. Smith, on Oliver Street. Here he was the subject of one of those inhuman practices which disgrace this class of business in nearly all ports. Desiring to "have a little run ashore" before he went to sea again, he paid his landlord for two weeks board in advance. In about four days the landlord came to him and said: "Bill, I want you to go in a little down-east bark to New Orleans, and then up the Mediterranean." Bill declined, as he had been ashore so short a time, and had paid for his board in advance, and he did not wish to go to sea so soon again. Little did Mr. Smith care for that. He sent one of his "runners" to entice Bill down to one of the "chain lockers," and there he was persuaded to take a couple of "drinks," which stupefied him, and when he came to he found himself in a "Whitehall" boat, with his "dunnage," and shipped on the bark bound for New Orleans under another name than his own. One of the men engaged by Smith to the captain of the bark had decided not to go, and this method was taken to supply his place with Mr. Fletcher. However, he left the bark in New Orleans and shipped on board a large Philadelphia ship for Liverpool. After the cargo of this ship was discharged, six hundred emigrants were taken aboard for Philadelphia. In running down the channel, when off Holyhead, and before all the emigrants had gone below, a fearful squall struck the ship and away went the three topmasts, the jib-boom and all the "top-hamper" of the vessel with them over the side. When the wreckage was cleared away, about day-light, one of the Belfast steamers picked up the ship and towed her to that port. Here Mr. Fletcher left her, returned to Liverpool and en-tered on another ship bound for New York.

On arriving in New York he went up to see his old "friend" Smith, who was "delighted" to see him, and desired immediately to send for his "dun-nage," which was yet on the ship. Mr. Fletcher declined, reminding Smith in not very gentle words of the "dirty trick" he had played him be-fore, and took up his quarters at "Jack Barry's," at 42 Cherry street. But a like experience await-ed him here, for, in about a week he was again outward bound for San Francisco in the ship Monument, of New York. The ship had a stormy passage, but arrived in San Francisco about the last of March, 1850.

By this time Mr. Fletcher was becoming wearied of the sea, or, if not of the sea itself, then of the character of the life that comes to the ordinary sailor. And, besides, this was in the very midst of the golden flood of prosperity that was rolling over San Francisco, and over all the Pacific coast, from the gold mines that had been discovered but about two years before. Wages were so high and work so abundant that he determined to try what he could do on shore. Stopping in San Francisco and working along shore for some time. the enchanting tales of sudden and fabulous wealth to be dug out of the hills and gulches of the Sierra Nevadas drew him away from the city, and he soon found himself on Feather River, and engaged in mining on a bar on the Middle Fork of that stream, in the primitive fashion of that primitive period. Himself and his companion generally took from the dirt from twenty to thirty dollars per day. The winter was spent in the southern mines, where the same fortune attended his work. Notwithstanding money was so rapidly and easily made. it was just as rapidly and easily spent. Still he wrought industriously on until the fall of 1853. when he sold out his interest in the mines on Feather River, went down to San Francisco and shipped for Liverpool. with the intention of visiting his mother in Ireland and his sister in New York. and then returning to California. But though he visited the place of his nativity. which he had left when a mere boy, he found that his mother had removed to England and so he did not see her.

By this time, it is clearly to be seen, Mr. Fletcher had come to some enlarged views of the purposes and ends of life. He had seen its hard sides and dark shadows. He had visited many of the great ports of the world. Sea and land were familiar to him. His body was hardened by toil, his mind expanded by trial, and to a good degree aspiration for a better condition of life was awakened in his soul. One can easily trace these results in the record he made of the events and experiences of these years. Still there is not, up to this time, a single intimation of any religious emotion or sentiment coming into his heart or fashioning his purposes. Still there was love in his heart; love to his friends, affection for mother and sister, and an evident desire to minister to their happiness. Where there is any susceptibility for love, there is yet a place for God in any human heart. This has evidently been a growing grace in the heart of Mr. Fletcher up to this time.

Not finding his mother, the young man turned back again towards his sister, who was still residing in New York. He had got beyond the hard need of working his way before the mast, and took passage on the steamship "City of Glasgow," with a large company of passengers. This was the last trip of that ill-fated vessel. On her next voyage she sailed out of her port with a large passenger list, disappeared in the sky-rimmed loneliness of the ocean, and was never heard of more.

Remaining with his sister a few days in New York, he returned to California and its golden treasures. So prospered was he in his mining operations that in the fall of 1854, finding that he had $2,000 for his summer's work, he resolved to return to New York and spend the winter with his sister in that city. But life even in a great city, lacked the excitement and impulse of life in the

mines and mountains of California, so, in the spring
of 1855, taking his sister with him, he turned his
face again towards the west, and, after a short
tarry in San Francisco, with his sister he went into
Klamath County, California, and again began mining at Sawyer's Bar, on Salmon River.

There is something in the work of mining for
gold that holds an adventurous and enthusiastic
spirit with an entrancing grip.   It seems monotonous to a looker on, but not so to the worker.   The
excitement of seeking something that is only just
out of sight, and that something gold;   and the
hope that the next blow of the pick or the next
pitch of the shovel will uncover it to the eager
gaze, keeps the nerves strung to rapid and easy
toil.   And in those early days the weirdness and
wildness of the mountain gorges, the rush and roar
of the river, the song and shout of the successful
miners, the lights of the campfires that set aglow
the hillsides, the "yarns" of the eager circle that
drew near the cheering blaze, the stories of "finds"
of fabulous wealth in some distant camp that seemed to breath themselves over plains and mountains and through forests for hundreds of miles to
every miner's cabin, all conspired to spread over

such a life a charm and a promise that were unknown and unfelt in city or on farm. It was a new
civilization, if it was civilization, or a new barbarism, if it were a barbarism. If it were either, it
had many of the elements of the other strongly
blended with its own, and so constituted a new
life, rough but charming, developing a character
of strong vigor, of high independence, with a kind
of wild, penetrating intelligence that could look
farther into a rock for a seam of gold than any
other time or people have ever evolved. Out of
this new civilized-barbarism have developed many
of the strongest and most practical intellects of
our national history. Out of it have come many
of the purest and most chivalrous Christian lives
that have blessed humanity. Amidst it have been
kindled to immortal song poetic spirits that else
had dreamed themselves away in unsung rhap-
sodies amidst the monotonous and uninspiring
bricks and walls of the dreary cities, or in measur-
ing calicos and woolseys behind the counters of village traders. There is a relation of beauty and
poetry between true souls and Sierra heights up
there in the skies, and murmuring cascades and

flowing rivers in the gorges and on the plains. Since Bryant sung of

"Where rolls the Oregon,
And hears no sound save his own dashings."

till Miller glorified the mountain peaks of California with the "Song of the Sierras," it has been thus.

Mr. Fletcher remained at Sawyer's Bar as a miner until the fall of 1858, when he removed a few miles to a place known as "Russian Creek," where he secured interests in mining property and applied himself with his usual industry to the hard toil of the miner. Nothing of special note occurred in his life or fortune during the first year that he spent on Russian Creek. He had a home kept by his sister, whom he cherished very fondly and faithfully, and the months of daily toil in the mines during the summer of 1859 were pleasant. His lot seemed fixed for life. He had drifted off the ocean and drifted, almost without purpose, into the mountains of California. But life has its eras, many of them seemingly beyond our own ordering, but it may be guided by a wiser and more powerful hand than our own.   So it may prove with Mr. Fletcher.

CHAPTER II.

THE CHANGED LIFE.

"That which is born of the flesh is flesh; and that which is born of the Spirit is spirit. Marvel not that I said unto thee, ye must be born again."—Jesus.

THE life that Mr. Fletcher had lived up to the fall of 1859 was, as we have seen, that of a seafarer and miner. While such a life had in it much that would prove detrimental and even ruinous to a man of weak moral nature, to one of a vigorous sense of the reality of life there was in it an experience that could be made very effective and useful in the future. A wide knowledge of the world, and a wide acquaintance with all classes and conditions of men, gained by personal contact with them, was a kind of education that compensated in a good measure for the lack of the education of the schools. None have greater opportunities for acquiring such knowledge than the sailor and the miner. They see men at their best and at their worst. They become acquainted with the kindest and noblest of men, and with the hardest and meanest. They meet and mingle with the most truly religious and the most shockingly wicked. They hear prayers and profanity in the same company. Drunkenness reels and staggers before them or lies down and wallows in the mire of the gutter, and sobriety walks with manly uprightness and clean garb at the same time. They see the difference; and the man of natural moral strength instinctively comes to choose the better for his portion. The lesson may not always be learned quickly, but it is quite sure to be finally learned. It may not always be learned radically, so as to lead to a distinctively religious life, but it will often be so; and when it is it makes a character that becomes a worthy model of life. This was the result with Mr. Fletcher.

He had now reached thirty years of age. His naturally sincere mind had been prepared in many ways for the planting of the seed of truth within it, and when it was once planted it could rapidly spring up into a gracious harvest. The instrumentality that finally reached this result was simple, yet "mighty through God."

In the autumn of 1859 a religious friend by the name of Henry Ferrett made a visit to the mining camp of Mr. Clough and Fletcher, and spent the evening in a religious conversation with Mr. Clough, Mr. Fletcher being a simple listener. He had never read the Bible. He had never attended religious meetings. His naturally inquisitive mind detected at once that Mr. Ferrett was in possession of something to which he was a stranger. On retiring for the night, after a chapter of the Word of God had been read by Mr. Clough, Mr. Ewing made an earnest prayer that God would apply the truth about which they had been talking to the hearts of all present. Mr. Fletcher says:

"It was the first time I had knelt in prayer for many, many years. I then and there gave my heart to God, and asked Him to teach me how to pray and lead me in the way of truth. The few little prayers I had learned when I was a child, out of our Catholic prayer book, I believe, since God has shown me the way of truth, were not in harmony with God's word."

To the truth that makes "wise unto salvation" Mr. Fletcher was an utter stranger up to this time. All about him were like himself. His closest associates were irreligious. His own sister, his brother-in-law, his daily companions, all alike forgot

God. It was under such unfavorable surroundings that then and there Mr. Fletcher's mind and
heart reached the high resolve to surrender to
God. The way, the time, the completeness of his
resolve and the deliberate earnestness of his action
under it, mark the inherent independence and sincerity of his nature, as well as the reality of his
change "from darkness to light." He says of it:

"I did not experience that joy and ecstacy which some
have felt, but I felt an abiding witness of the Spirit of God
in my soul that He had pardoned my sins and accepted
me as righteous in His sight for the sake of Christ."

How thoroughly this work of regeneration
changed the course and purpose as well as the motive and spirit of his life is expressed in his own
record of the event. He says:

"I then commenced to strive to read His word, for I had
no one to teach me but God. How many times I went on
my knees and spread my Bible before the Lord, and there
spelt out the word, for I could not read. But the Lord,
who is more willing to give than I was to ask Him, gave me
that light by which I was enabled to read His word in a
short time, and also how to write, so that all I am I owe
to the goodness of God towards me."

One can hardly imagine less favorable conditions for the development of the religious and in-

tellectual life of a man like Mr. Fletcher than those that surrounded him at this time. The trueness and decision of his action alienated his old friends, and they "went by on the other side." But their loss was his gain. God did not forsake him, but raised up other and better friends; for He never leaves himself without a witness to those that seek Him. Not long after his conversion he was minded by the Divine Spirit, to visit the family of a Mr. Reany. During the visit Mrs. Reany spoke most earnestly about seeking the Saviour, and finding his heart inclined that way, encouraged him in every way she could. Among other helps she gave him two of the books that have helped mould the Christian life of thousands, namely, Bunyan's Pilgrim's Progress, and Dodridge's Rise and Progress of Religion in the Soul. These were the first religious books he ever read; and these were read when he was only able to read at all by the laborious spelling out of each individual word. After he had thus read them once he took them back to their owner with the acknowledgment that he could not understand them. She persuaded him to take them back and read them again; and herself gave him some instructions

how to read them understandingly. He took
them again, read them over more carefully, earnestly praying to God to enlighten his mind so that
he could understand them. The prayer was answered, and he was greatly blessed then, and
through all his life, by this ministry of these two
eminent and devoted men, long after they had
gone to Heaven.

Mrs. Reany so illustrates a phase of the frag-
mentary religious life found in mining regions, and
on the frontiers, that we should not pass by this
incident without a brief notice of it. Mr. Fletcher speaks of her most tenderly and gratefully. Her
interest in him religiously led to inquiry concerning her, when he found "she was a member of the
Methodist Episcopal Church at Saywyer's Bar;
a good, pious woman, one who was always striving
to lead sinners into the light and liberty of the children of God." This good woman evidently became "the guide, philosopher and friend" of Mr.
Fletcher in his earliest Christian life, and, without
a doubt, her influence and teaching did much to
fashion that life that ripened into such a beautiful
fruitage in later years. His own brief reference to

this early Christian friendship is so tender and
frank that we here transcribe it. He says:

"I was living seven miles from her place of residence, so
I had not many opportunities of speaking to her. When I
would go to see her the first question she would ask me
was how I was getting along spiritually. She won my confidence and I opened my mind to her freely. O, how the
tears ran from her eyes when I told her of my resolve to
serve God and make my way to heaven. She then invited
me to join her little class and become a member of her
church. I told her when I came down again I would let
her know about it. In the meantime I was striving to read
my Bible, but could not read it very well yet; though the
Lord was giving me light and liberty in it.

"The next time I went to Sawyer's Bar was in April,
1860. It was on Sunday, and I met Mrs. Reany going to
hold her Bible class and class meeting. I asked her what
that meant. She told me if I would go with her I would
find out for myself. I thank God I did find out one thing. I
found out that it was more profitable for me to be there
than to spend the hours in the saloon or bar-room. When
the little meeting was over Mrs. Reany told me that their
Presiding Elder would be there on the twelfth of May to
hold their quarterly meeting, and asked me to attend it. I
told her that I would be down and hear a Methodist
preacher for the first time in my life. I spent the time before the quarterly meeting reading my Bible and improving
my mind. I made some inquiries about the doctrines and
discipline of the Methodist Church, and made up my mind
to become a member of that church at the coming quarterly meeting.

"As I was about to join another church than that under which I was brought up, I put myself under the guidance of God, to be led by Him, for He had assured me in His Word if I would acknowledge Him in all my ways, that He would direct my paths.

"May the eleventh, I left home to attend the quarterly meeting, and on May 12th, 1860, at Sawyer's Bar, on Salmon River, Klamath County, California, I joined the Methodist Episcopal Church on probation, under Nelson Reasoner, presiding elder of the Mount Shasta District, California Conference."

Mr. Fletcher concludes this touching account of his early Christian life up to his union with the visible church with an earnest prayer for grace and guidance in the life he had thus and there undertaken, and solemnly records his vow of fidelity as a member of that church with which he had connected himself. How he kept that vow will appear in the entire course of this narrative.

It appears a strange coincidence that the Rev. Nelson Reasoner, under whose ministry Mr. Fletcher became a member of the Methodist Episcopal Church, should have been one of the most intimate of the early ministerial friends of the writer of these memoirs, when we were both in our early twenties in Western New York. We have not met for nearly fifty years, but our works thus

meet in the actual and recorded life of our dear
Brother Fletcher, thousands of miles distant from
where our early associations were formed.

Thus the wandering, wayward life of William
S. Fletcher, after being tossed by the storms of all
the seas so long, and buffeted and beaten by so
many waves and adverse tides, came to safe anch-
orage at last, and he could joyously sing:

My soul in sad exile was out on life's sea,
    So burdened with sin and distress.
Till I heard a sweet voice saying make me your choice,
    And I entered the haven of rest.

I've anchored my soul in the haven of rest,
    I'll sail the wide seas no more;
The tempest may sweep o'er the wild stormy deep;
    In Jesus I'm safe evermore.

Here in the fastnesses of the mountains this
rover from the seas found this safety; and, with a
little band of eight, who there represented the
great Church of Christ on the earth, connected
himself as a Christian. As these eight names had
such a vital relation to the after life of Mr. Fletcher, we transcribe them from his journal: Joseph
Beasley, leader; Henry Ferrett, E. Lee. Joseph
Smith, Josiah Gwin, Mrs. Reany, Mrs. Luckett
and W. S. Fletcher.

It will be interesting and profitable to trace the early Christian life of Mr. Fletcher, while he remained in this locality, a little farther. His helpers were very few in number, though these few were men and women of good sense and solid character. They had no pastor, and only once in three months were favored with a visit from the Presiding Elder of whom we have spoken. But the means of grace, like class meetings, Bible class, prayer meeting, were not neglected. Mr. Fletcher lost no opportunity for improvement in knowledge, as well as in piety. Immediately on his conversion an impulse to do good to others became the controlling force of his mind. Small as was the light kindled in his heart, and few as there were among the rough miners of the mountains to profit by it, it was never hid under a bushel. There is a charming simplicity and honesty in the words in which he himself wrote of his first participation in public religious services. It was not long after he had connected himself with the church. He says:

"Our class leader gave out an appointment for a prayer meeting in connection with our class meeting. As it was the first prayer meeting that I had ever attended, and the first that had ever been held in our class since I united with it. I did not know how I should get through with it. I had never prayed in public, and was greatly troubled during the week to know how I should act. I wrote a little prayer for the coming meeting and committed it to memory. It was well fixed in my mind, as I hardly thought of anything else during the week. When Sabbath evening came and our meeting time drew near I was very much embarrassed about my little prayer. Although I could repeat it readily, I felt that I had not confidence in myself. As our meeting progressed I scarcely knew what was going on, as my mind was so taken up with my little prayer. The class leader called on me to pray. As I was in the act of kneeling my little prayer vanished from my mind. As quick as thought it came into my mind to ask God to be my present help in time of need. Blessed be God! I prayed in a way I had never prayed before. I had an access to the throne of grace I had never had before. This is the second time the Lord has taught me not to put too much confidence in my own strength, and I have profited, I trust, by my own experiences, to trust more in God and less in myself."

Thus early, while he was yet only a probationer in the church, this uneducated young miner began to evince that sturdy honesty of purpose and whole-hearted consecration to God which marked, as the reader will see, all his career, and made his life so widely useful to lost men.

The long mountain winters come early in these rugged ranges where the miner seeks for gold..

Hence the last visit of the Presiding Elder to Sawyer's Bar for 1860 came in October. Mr. Fletcher notes the date—October 26th—as the time he first partook of "The Supper of the Lord." He speaks of it most devoutly and prays "may God cleanse me from sin and make me a partaker of His divine nature." Incidentally, in the same entry in his journal in which he records this incident, he refers to another fact that shows his intense thirst for knowledge as well as religious experience. It will be remembered that before his conversion to God, only six months before this time, he could neither read nor write. During this fall he purchased Clarke's Commentaries, six very large volumes, one of the most learned works that the world had ever seen when they were published, paying for them $22.00. During all that long winter he "improved every opportunity in reading them." In reviewing this time he says:

"I hope the light I have received from these books will never be blotted out of my memory. I now begin to feel the want of education. All that I know God has taught me since I gave Him my heart. He has enabled me to read and write, and above all He has taught me how to live; and I have a reasonable hope that when my proba-

tionary life is over He will receive me to His everlasting
Kingdom to praise Him forever in Heaven."

On May 12, 1861, Mr. Fletcher was admitted
to "full connection" in the Methodist Episcopal
Church by Rev. Nelson Reasoner, who had admitted him upon probation exactly one year before.
His own reflections on this occasion open the
door of his heart as nothing we could write would,
and will give the reader a clear insight into the
true philosophy of his life. He writes:

"In looking over this the first year of my Christian experience, my heart feels humbly thankful to God for His
merciful care over me. When I look back and see what I
was before I gave God my heart, and then see what I am
now, surely my soul is grateful to God for taking 'my feet
out of the miry clay and establishing my goings and
putting a new song in my mouth, even praises to my God.'
He has caused the light to shine out of darkness, and He
hath shined in my heart to give me the light of the knowledge of the glory of God in the grace of Jesus Christ. My
prayer to God is that I may be perfected in love and filled
with all the fullness of God."

At this time the Presiding Elder introduced Mr.
Fletcher to a new and wider field of Christian influence. He organized a Sabbath School, and
though Mr. Fletcher had never been in one in his
life, appointed him a teacher. It was not Mr.

Fletcher's way to decline opportunities for doing good, and so he readily entered this open door, and took charge of a most interesting class of girls. There was an excellent library of books in connection with the school, and these Mr. Fletcher himself read with his usual care and attention. Useful as he was to his class, his work in the school was scarcely less useful to himself. He learned the blessedness of doing good as he had never learned it before. Giving, he received. Strengthening others, he was strengthened. Leading others in the right way, he was led in it himself. He was never slow to learn this lesson, and the effect of it, as we shall see, remained with him ever after. Fortified by his year's advancing experience in the things of God and in the work of God, he came into the early summer of 1862 only to meet more trying difficulties than any that he had hitherto encountered.

It was characteristic of Mr. Fletcher that he had a "fixed heart." He was never unstable. If ever a man could adopt the words of the Psalmist without reserve, "O God, my heart is fixed," that man was W. S. Fletcher. It was the element that made him. One feels a holy pride of humanity

itself when he studies such a Christian, however
humble his accidental sphere in life. It is the
heart of all true greatness. It is the sure prophet
of victory, whether on the highways or in the by-
ways of life.

The trials that came to Mr. Fletcher in the summer of 1862 were in no wise of a personal nature,
but related solely to the condition of the work of
God in the small community in which he took so
deep an interest. The Sabbath school in which
he was a teacher began to decline. Superinten-
dent, teachers and even the pastor forsook it, until Mr. Fletcher and his class were all that remained. Faithful among the faithless and discour-
aged, he sought the advice and encouragement of
the pastor, but he met discouragement rather.
He declared his purpose to continue it unless his
own class deserted him. The pastor advised him
to "dry it up." Mr. Fletcher appointed a meeting
for the afternoon of Sunday. Every member of
his class, seventeen in all, was present. He di-
vided the class; gave one to each of two girls
fourteen years of age, taking the superintendency
himself. This prompt and faithful action on
the part of Mr. Fletcher saved the Sunday school,

and continued this instrumentality of grace among
these scattered and needy children of the mountains. It was characteristic of the man; such a
spirit as has marked the work of his whole life.
He records this as the most trying week of his
experience up to this time, but it brought him its
usual compensating lesson, namely, "not to trust
too much in others if I want to make progress in
holiness of heart and life."

Thus amidst the solitudes of this mining gulch,
the work of God was carried on and the standard
of the cross upheld, and mainly by the instrumentality of this one man; not yet two years rescued
from the bondage of sin; and now only just started on that career of usefulness which has given
him such a warm place in the hearts of thousands
on the sea and on the land. An incident will
show the gentle yet decided force with which
he asserted his Christian principles and vindicated
his Christian liberty among his mining companions in these proverbially ungodly associations.

In one of his mining ventures on "White's
Gulch" he accepted a partner who was a very profane man. Mr. Fletcher reasoned with him about
the folly and wickedness of his course, and then

told him that he was a member of the Methodist
church and had made his house a house of prayer;
and if he came to live with him he would have to
conform to the rules of his home. This decisive
course was effective. The man came, and within
a few weeks became himself a member of the
church. At this place there had been almost literally no religious influence or sentiment until Mr.
Fletcher came into the church. Others, among
whom were some of those who had been associated
with him at Sawyer's Bar, came afterwards. As
winter came on he went through the camp, looking up all those who desired to live a Christian life,
called them together at his "old cabin," and
though there were but few of them, and only "five
outsiders who used to attend these meetings," organized and kept up an "old fashioned prayer
meeting" all winter. Some were converted; among
them a Frenchman, a Catholic, by the name of
Nichols, who was unable to speak English, and
used to pray and speak in his own language, while
the great tears rolled down his face and best be-
spoke his gratitude to God for deliverance from
the double bondage of sin and the superstitions of
Catholicism.

During this winter strong efforts were made by the Catholic priest to break up the Sabbath school under Mr. Fletcher's superintendence. Some Catholic children attended it, and were becoming greatly interested in it, and especially in the reading of the Sunday School Advocate. This he forbade them to read, and denounced all who read it as heretics. Mr. Fletcher, in his usual open and frank way went directly to the parents of the children and inquired if they objected to their children attending, the school and reading the papers They replied that they did not. He then encouraged them to come, gave them the papers, and, unawed and unashamed, went straight forward in his "work of faith and labor of love."

CHAPTER III.

TO A NEW FIELD.

"It is often reserved for 'every-day people,' as we are apt to call them, to illustrate one of the facts of life—that a crisis produces the man to meet it."—Gustav Kobe.

MR. FLETCHER'S work seemed now to be done in the mountains of California. Providence appeared to be calling him to a far northern field. He had been thrown upon the golden coast, a waif of the seas, almost without purpose, and wholly without a large and noble aim in life. He appeared to others, and probably to himself, like one of the vast multitude of human beings who, as tramps of the land and rovers of the ocean, existed only to wander in aimless disquietude of being, wherever the momentary whim or the chance currents of impulse might take them, and then to die out on the desert sands, or deep in the mountain gorges, or on the restless tides of the never quiet seas, and be buried out of sight and thought of their more favored, or more highly endowed human fellows. Three decades of life had thus gone, more than one of which had been spent in California at a time that witnessed the utter moral and intellectual wreck of more men in proportion to the population of the State than ever occurred in any other land in the same length of time. Who could have prophesied that this uneducated Irish boy should wring, out of that hard lot, the elements of a character that should make him in the next thirty years such an honored instrument of good to so many people as he became. If he did not dig much gold out of the gulches of these California mountains he did dig out of them that which was better than gold. All this turned on a single fact, namely, that he was wise enough to respond to the call of God to His love and service at almost the first time that call ever came to him; and that he kept himself open to that call of God, and lived "obedient to the heavenly vision" that then, as we have shown, rose upon his soul.

It was in July, 1863, that Mr. Fletcher decided to leave California, and turn his face towards far Northern Idaho. He felt it was God's will; why, he

could not tell; where it would lead him he did not
know. Tender and touching was his farewell to
his little Sunday school in the mountains. Great
their regrets in bidding him farewell. Among
them was one, especially, of whom we have spoken
before as his "guide, philosopher and friend," in
the beginning of his Christian life: Mrs. Reany.
Probably she little understood the far reach of her
good work in leading him to Christ; but still
there must have been a sensitive chord quivering
in her heart when she bade him good-bye. Mr.
Fletcher records his gratitude to God and to those
with whom he had lived and labored in very tender
terms; and at the same time expresses his deep regret that he "had not had some one to lead him to
Jesus in the days of his youth."

His sister and her husband had been living with
or near him, in the mines for some years. They
were not only unconverted, but had been violently
opposed to the religious life of their brother.
With a fidelity and tenderness that was wonderful,
he had counseled and besought them to give their
hearts to God. He had been to his sister more
than brother; father, provider and friend, but she
flung his counsel to the mountain winds and

turned away from his God and Saviour. When he was to leave her in this great wild of loneliness and sin the memory of his kindness, of his faithfulness, of his love, overcame her stubborn heart, and she promised him in the last words she then spoke to him, that she would "give her heart to God and join our church." With this new benediction on his soul he turned away and went out, "not knowing whither he went."

On leaving the narrow field where he had so faithfully striven to do all that came to him in the work of the Master, Mr. Fletcher joined the great movement of the mining population of the Pacific coast northward towards the newly opened mining regions of Washington and Idaho Territories. Industrious, provident and frugal, although his mining adventures had not brought him great wealth, they had not left him in that abject poverty that has been the result with such multitudes of the men who, like himself, entered upon them without the education and moral training that enabled them to cope with the trained rascality of the gamblers and saloon keepers who laid their plans of knavery and robbery for every unwary visitor. From such a fate he was rescued by his religion,

without which the name of W. S. Fletcher would
have perished with the unnumbered multitudes
that went down unknown and unregretted in the
gulches of California and in the mountains of Idaho. For this reason alone, when he left California,
he left amidst the benedictions and tears and prayers of those who loved him; those whom he loved.
If he did not carry much gold with him on his
journey, he carried golden memories far better
than gold. Yet he went in comfort, and his journey northward became the means of shaping the
ultimate field of his true life work.

The incident on his journey to the north which
most aided him in that which was always
uppermost in his mind—his religious life—was
the falling providentially into the company
of Bishop E. S. Janes, one of the sweetest,
most beloved and useful bishops of his own
church. At Yreka, California, where he spent
the first Sabbath after he left his old home,
the Bishop preached; and from Yreka to Oregon was his traveling companion in the close
fellowship of a stage-coach. Those who knew the
tenderness and simplicity of the Bishop's manner
and the sweet and insinuating method of his con-

versation in private, will understand how quickly
and completely he would win the confidence and
trust of such a heart as Mr. Fletcher's. Nor would
the eager, sympathising attention of the latter to
everything said intended or adapted to benefit a
hearer, fail to draw forth from the good Bishop all
his good natured efforts to benefit the listener.
Like all really great and good men, the Bishop was
not pretentious, either in garb or manners, but
plain and direct; always affable, always kind.
Probably the week spent in this journey in this
coach with the Bishop, with the opportunity it
brought Mr. Fletcher, of observing the spirit and
listening to the conversation and sharing the advice of this truly godly man and most able Bishop,
did as much as any one week of his life to elevate
and ennoble his conception of true manhood and
consecrated piety. And when the same bishop visited Oregon again, many years after, Mr. Fletcher met him and re-called to him the incident of this
ride together through the mountains of Northern
California and Southern Oregon, and inquired if
he "remembered the little Irishman who was his
traveling companion on the journey." "O yes,"
replied the venerable man, "and I have often and

always thought of you in connection with that trip." So this humble young miner and this exalted Bishop of the church were a mutual ministry of help and pleasure by the way.

From Portland, which was reached August 7th, and where one Sabbath was spent, improved, as was usual with him, in attendance on all the services of the house of God, Mr. Fletcher pursued his journey for "Bannock City," Idaho, where he arrived on the 31st of August, 1863.

"Bannock City," later and now known as "Idaho City," was one of the richest mining camps ever discovered on the Pacific slope. It is located in the far interior, in the very top of the Salmon River range of mountains, about thirty-five miles north of the present "Boise City," the beautiful Capital of the now State of Idaho. It was a place of awful wickedness. The vagrants, the gamblers, the thieves, the murderes and the prostitutes, who had been driven away from the older mining towns of the coast on account of their crimes, had all gathered in these Idaho mountains, where they organized a pandemonium of crime. They reigned for a long time supreme. They organized society in the interest of crime, and for the protection of criminals. They elected civil officers for the same purpose. Sheriffs were bandits, and treasurers were thieves. Bannock City at that time was a real Aceldama, "the field of blood." Never before, and probably never since, even in mining camps, was there a more desperate body of men gathered in one place.

Probably, however, in the very worst mining communities of the coast some of the very best men are found. Indeed, where the worst of the bad prevail, the best of the good are found, for God never leaves Himself without a witness. So it was in this place, and ultimately, here as elsewhere, the few righteous proved themselves more than a match for the many wicked, and gradually restored society to the conditions of civilization known in other places. The writer for many years subsequently visited "Idaho City," officially in the work of his ministry, and found quietude where there had been storm; peace and safety where there had been robbery and murder.

In the work of rescuing the place from its dark pall of wrong and sin Mr. Fletcher was the pioneer. Those who have followed us thus far in the incidents of his life would not expect he would enter

even such a place as this, and not let his light shine
forth.   Almost before he had struck his miner's
pick into the gravel he makes this record:

"The week after I came here I started out to hunt up
some of our members, for I knew that there must be many
of them here, but I could find only four on my first round.
I got them to promise that they would meet me the next
Sabbath evening at the Colorado House for a class and
prayer meeting. They came, and we had a most refreshing season. As far as I can find out this was the first
prayer and class meeting that has been held in this place."

Undoubtedly to Mr. Fletcher belongs the hon-
or of thus gathering into an organization the first
band of Christian workers in those Idaho mountains.   But he was soon followed by others, and
about three months after this small organization
was effected, Rev. C. S. Kingsley, a very able minister from Portland, Oregon, reached the place,
and entered at once on the work of organizing a
society and erecting a house of worship. He highly approved the work done by Mr. Fletcher, and
from that time forward they earnestly co-operated
in the work before them. By May, 1864, a church
was completed and opened, a class of twelve members organized, and a Sunday school established,
and thus the institutions of Christianity were per-

manently erected in Idaho City. In all this work Mr. Fletcher was a chief instrument.

There was little of special incident attending the work in which Mr. Fletcher was engaged in Idaho during the remainder of the time of his residence there; which was until late in September, 1864. He did, what is the most difficult of all things for a Christian to do, "always abounded in the work of the Lord." In his mining claim, where he toiled from day to day, in the prayer and class meetings, at which he was always present, on the highway where he walked with the multitude, in the places of trade, everywhere and always he was the gentle, kindly man; the devoted, self-denying Christian. Trials were borne with resignation; labors performed with intelligent trust; and his open hand ever had its gift of charity for the needy, or his contribution to help forward the work of God. When the time came that he felt God's call to him was elsewhere, he sold out his mining claim, adjusted all his temporal affairs with conscientious faithfulness, ready to go where God had work for him to do most to glorify Himself. Under date of September 2nd he makes this entry:

"As this is the last time I intend to be with the children

in the Sabbath school. I spoke to them about loving their Saviour, especially to my own class. May the good seed that has been sown bring forth abundant fruit in their young hearts to the glory of God. I feel greatly thankful to God for His assisting grace which has enabled me to prove faithful to my calling which is in Christ Jesus during my sojourn in this wicked place. I can say from an honest heart that I have grown in grace and in the knowledge of the truth as it is in Jesus since I came here, and as I intend leaving this place to-morrow for Portland and San Francisco, and if it is the Lord's will, for Ireland, I desire above all things to acknowledge God in all my ways, that he may direct my paths."

These reflections and this prayer are in harmony with all he did and all he felt from the moment of his conversion. He kept God in all his thoughts, and God kept and cared for him in all his ways.

His journey to Portland and thence to San Francisco via Victoria, was without noteworthy incident. In San Francisco he immediately connected himself with the church of which Jesse T. Peck, D. D., afterwards Bishop, was pastor. Here he had the satisfaction of seeing his sister, who had promised him at Sawyer's Bar, when he was about to leave for Idaho, that she would become a Christian and unite herself with the Methodist Church, give her name also as a probationer to the church.

What seemed to him the special work God would now have for him to do was to care for the religious and intellectual improvement of that beloved sister. He proved his real manhood by the care he took of her. He met her on his arrival in San Francisco, surrounded by influences greatly adverse to her spiritual and intellectual well being, but he immediately put her into the Santa Clara Female Collegiate Institute, under the family care of Rev. Mr. Tuthill and lady, where all her interests were tenderly and faithfully cared for; himself paying all bills for tuition and board. This, he felt, was his special call to California. Though he came to San Francisco with his mind fully disposed to ship for Ireland, yet he found that the providence of God had closed that way to him, and, as ever, he said "Thy will be done." When all his arrangements for his sister's welfare were made and he was about to leave her again, he says in his journal:

"The few days I have spent with her have been a bright spot in my life. I have been enabled by the grace of God to sacrifice my own pleasure in giving up the idea of going to Ireland to spend the winter, in order that I might make my sister more comfortable and happy. Our parting this time has been most affectionate. Her heart seems to be touched by the power of God. I feel very lonely in leaving her, not knowing where I shall go; but I am determined to go wherever the Lord shall direct, for He will direct me aright."

He returned to San Francisco, where the impression was forcibly made upon his mind that he should go back to Portland, Oregon. To him it was a heavenly vision, and immediately he was obedient to it, and on the 29th of October, 1864, he took passage on the steamer for that place, arriving there on the first day of November, 1864.

Though Mr. Fletcher had now reached the place where was to be wrought the great work of his life, he was not yet to enter upon it. All his previous experiences, both before and after his conversion, had been preparatory to it. But there were yet other preparations to which God was bringing him as he was made able to bear them. The careless reader might suppose, as he has followed him in his rovings on the sea and his journeyings on the land; in his mingling with sailors on the decks of vessels and in the many ports to which he sailed; as he dug in the mines of California and Idaho, that he was but one of the floating thousands whose employments were like his, who were ever saying. "Let us eat and drink, for to-morrow we die;" mere floating fragments of humanity, not thinking what they were nor whither they were drifting. Now in Ireland, now in England, now in America; one month in Galway, the next in Liverpool, the next in New York, the next in San Francisco; what was there in that to prepare an uneducated man for any great mission of after life, or to qualify him to reach and influence other lives on a broad and efficient scale? God knew, and "God disposes;" and He made all these things work together for the good both of Mr. Fletcher himself and the world through him.

On his arrival in Portland in the begining of the winter of 1864-5, he immediately connected himself with Taylor Street Church, then under the pastorate of Rev. David Rutledge, and entered heartily into its work. With this change there had come to him the thought of a home, so he purchased a plat of ten acres of land of Rev. Albert Kelly, in whose family he boarded, and with his usual industry set to work to clear and improve it. In the midst of his manual toil, such as clearing and grubbing land and building a house, he began the reading of the New Testament through

by course, while on his knees looking for God's
blessing to be upon the word to sanctify his own
soul. He also organized a Sabbath school in the
neighborhood where his home was located, a few
miles out of the city, and with a faithfulness that
was ever one of his most prominent characteris-
tics, attended all the services of the church and did
whatever came to his hands as a Christian in the
helping forward all that were about him. "To do
good and to communicate forget not;" which
Paul enjoined upon the early Christians, was the
very spirit of Mr. Fletcher's life. So he says:

"I can now see why the Lord brought me to this place.
Here are a few followers of His without any one to look
after them, with no class or prayer meetings, with preaching only once in four weks by our preacher in charge, who,
I must say, takes very little interest in us."

This religious indifference and spiritual destitution of the people bore heavily on his heart, and
he set to work to remedy it in his usual sensible
and practical way, by visiting among the people
religiously, holding prayer meetings and class
meetings and Sunday schools, and soon saw that
"his labor was not in vain in the Lord."

One cannot but wonder when he sees the results

of the work of this unpretending man in such lines
as these, why it should have remained for him almost alone of the vast multitudes in the church
everywhere his equals, and even his superiors in
general talents and education and even in opportunity, to demonstrate what one man alone can do
to further the cause of truth and piety among men.
But so it seemed to be in the places where his lot
was cast; but his faith and zeal never faltered and
God never ceased to honor his devotion. For two
years this character of work continued, while the
experience of Mr. Fletcher seemed like an ever
widening stream, flowing deeper and deeper, and
more and more enriching all the land. His careful and prayerful study of the Bible made him more
and more able to guide the people aright, and his
expositions of Scripture in prayer and class meetings and in occasional exhortations were often
accompanied by the power of the Holy Spirit.
Through his instrumentality the Lord added to
the church many that were saved, but beyond
this, and probably greater than this, during these
years of 1865 and 1866, with a part of 1867, these
labors and successes were a great help in the preparation of Mr. Fletcher himself for the new relig-

ious era that was now about to dawn on his own soul. He had learned well how to seize opportunity, and God gives the grace of opportunity to those who know how to use it.

CHAPTER IV.

THE HIGHER LIFE.

"Leaving the things that are behind and reaching forth to those things that are before."—Paul.

Take my soul and body's powers;
Take my memory, mind and will;
All my goods, and all my hours;
All I know and all I feel;
All I think, or speak, or do;
Take my heart, but make it new.

—Wesley

AS at the beginning of his Christian life, at the opening of what may be called its first era of experience, Mr. Fletcher deliberately, and in a clear business way, made a surrender of his heart to God, so when the years had taught him that there was a deeper experience and a larger life for him to enjoy and express, with the same deliberateness he moved forward to their attainment. This will be clearly seen from the following from his journal:

"Portland, March 27, 1867.

"I have this day consecrated myself anew to Jesus. I give Him all my sinful heart, rebellious will, my time and talents, and all that I possess, to be spent in His service. And now my blessed Jesus, I know that Thou wilt accept it, for I intend, God being my helper, never to take any of it back. I pray that I may be sanctified through the truth; for Thy Word is truth; and that I may adorn the doctrine of God my Saviour in all things.

WILLIAM S. FLETCHER."

The entrance of this record of his new and entire consecration to the service and work of his Redeemer is of such signal interest, and marks so decisively such an important era in his life, that it must be treated separate from the general story of that life. From the very beginning of his Christian experience he had been remarkably single hearted, and had always made his religion foremost in the purposes of his life. It is doubtful if he had forgotten to do this for a single moment, whether he was on the street, in the mines, in the church or at home. Still he had come to feel that there was a higher religious experience than he had enjoyed, and true to that prevailing purpose that distinguished him to reach the highest of which he was capable, he resolved to seek it.

Portland at this time was greatly stirred religiously under the preaching of Rev. A. B. Earle, a noted evangelist who was spending a few weeks in special revival work in the city. Mr. Fletcher's home was then a few miles out of the city, but on Sabbath, March 24th, he walked in to hear the evangelist, whose fame had filled all the region round about, preach. After hearing him, he determined to let his "work stop for a few days" and devote them especially to the services of Mr. Earle. The direct result to himself was the awakening in his heart of that intense desire for an advanced experience and a complete consecration of all his powers and life to God.

With Mr. Fletcher this was no spasmodic movement impelled by an excitement that might last but for a day, but the logical moral result of all his life since he became a Christian. Always "leaving the things that are behind he was reaching forward towards the things that are before," and "pressing towards the mark for the prize of the high calling of God in Christ Jesus." This was a moving up to the light that had come to him. The operations of his mind while coming up to it were of singular intensity and interest. We

follow them for a little, as the study of them may
help other inquiring and struggling souls.

In connection with his preaching, Mr. Earle
had put into the hands of those who heard him a
card containing a list of ten questions relating to
the personal religious life, as follows:

SELF EXAMINATION.

FOR OLDER CHRISTIANS.

1. Do I search my heart to the bottom, and act out its
convictions?

2. Do I believe I control my tongue and my temper?

3. Do I really believe the Bible is the law of my heart
and life?

4. Do I convince men that I believe there is an eternal
Hell?

5. Am I greatly concerned for the salvation of men?

6. Do I act like a Christian in my family and among my
intimate friends?

7. Do I fully believe I have been born again?

8. Do I know that I have power with God in prayer?

9. Do I believe I have been baptised with the Holy
Spirit since my conversion?

10. Am I sweetly resting in Christ by faith now?

These questions, covering the very heart of
Christian experience and life, could not but deep-

ly impress so sincere a mind as Mr. Fletcher's, and he quickly and fully resolved to test their widest reach of experimental and practical power.

Still he did not reach the point for which he aimed without a struggle. His record of it is plaintive and pathetic. Such words as "darkness," "no liberty," "struggle," "Satan using every means to draw me away," are the common terms by which he describes his emotions and feeling for some days after he had written the consecration paper at the head of this chapter, notwithstanding he attended the services of Mr. Earle all the time. Finally the conflict was ended in this way. He had attended a "meeting for holiness" in Taylor Street Church, Portland, without any special profit. On his return to his home he resolved to take up the next morning the ten questions proposed by Mr. Earle, and seek in special prayer the grace to answer them in the affirmative. This he did, most carefully and earnestly, while on his way to his work, a mile from his house; kneeling by the wayside in the woods, and reading them over on his knees, he accepted them all as the guide and test of his future Christian life. Still there were seasons of "restlessness," but

no real drawing back from his vows and faith of
consecration. The Scripture that led his mind out
at last into the ultimate trust was First John, first
chapter and seventh verse: "If we walk in the
light as he is in the light we have fellowship one
with another, and the blood of Jesus Christ his Son
cleanseth us from all sin." Now he was able to
say:—

> "Now rest, my long divided heart,
> Fixed on this blissful center, rest;
> Nor ever from thy Lord depart:—
> With Him of every good possest."

There in that struggle, alone with God in the
woods, he says:

"My axe which I held in my hand dropped harmless at
my side, and that beautiful hymn,—

> "There is a Fountain filled with blood,
> Drawn from Immanuel's veins;
> And sinners plunged beneath that flood,
> Lose all their guilty stains,"

spoke my faith. O, how my heart responded to the
words of my mouth! Blessed be God, I can now rejoice
evermore, pray without ceasing, and in everything give
thanks. 'Faithful is He that calleth me, who also will do
it.'"

Without doubt the mental and spiritual struggles of the last few days marked as distinct an era
in the life of Mr. Fletcher as did the date and
struggles of his first espousals. He had faithfully
used the grace first given and God entrusted to
him the larger riches. By the faithfulness and
growth of his earlier Christian life he had prepared
himself for the wider opportunities and greater
responsibilities that God had prepared for him in
his later life. Thus is it ever. God rewards faithfulness by larger trust, and compensates labor by
giving greater opportunities for labor.

But this victory of faith and this advanced experience in the divine life did not lift Mr. Fletcher
above the continued and faithful discharge of the
ordinary every-day duties of the Christian life. On
the contrary it gave a greater earnestness and a
deeper spirituality to that work. He not only
gave definite testimony to "what the Lord had
done for his soul," but in his place as a class leader,
and in all his relations as a Christian man seeking
to help God's children on in the heavenly way, and
to lead sinners to a knowledge of the truth he
walked and talked with greater freedom and enlargement. He not only attended the meetings

of his own class, but visited nearly all the classes
for many miles around, confirming and strengthening them in the fellowship of the faith of Jesus.
He made these visits on foot, and sometimes
walked fifteen or twenty miles in a day on these
missions of love. He did not assume to do this as
a teacher, but as a "brother beloved." He always
walked in an atmosphere of humility, and never
more so than after he had experienced the blessing
of "perfect love." He closes up the year 1867 with
many expressions of praise and gratitude to God
for His abounding mercy and goodness during the
year, especially in his "rich experience in spiritual
things." He makes this grateful record:—

"On the seventh day of last May the Lord sealed me for
His own. The impression that was then made on my poor
heart has grown stronger and brighter to the present moment; and now I can say from that experience that 'the
blood of Jesus Christ cleanseth me from all sin. O, how
humble it makes the soul to be freed from all the carnal
mind and to be filled with the love of Jesus!"

> O that the world would taste and see
> The riches of His grace;
> The arms of love that compass me
> Would all mankind embrace."

The early months of 1868 were marked by quite

an enlargement of the scope of Mr. Fletcher's
work. His singular influence in drawing the hearts
of those with whom he associated towards Christ,
and especially in leading believers into the higher
experiences of the Christian life, was becoming
widely understood, and his services were sought
for in many places. In his own class he was beloved as a brother, and he lavished his own love
upon them all. Within a circuit of twenty miles
from his home his kindly Christian influence was
strongly felt. Nor was that influence confined to
the rustic population of the hills and valleys amidst
which his own home lay; he was as welcome and
as beloved in the classess and Sunday schools of
the city as he was there. Not unfrequently he
would be with the classes in Portland in the morning and with those several miles distant in the afternoon, edifying believers, counseling unbeliev-
ers, speaking kindly to children, and by pureness
of life and charity of word "commending himself
to every man's conscience in the sight of God."
A record or two from his dairy will indicate the
constant character of his work at this time of his
life. On May 10th, 1868, he says:

"I attended the morning class in Portland, then heard

preaching, and then led the noon class, Brother Patterson being absent. I then came out and led my own class. I thank God for all the privileges I have enjoyed this Sabbath. May 11th. I went into the city to attend the Monday evening class. It was a feast to my soul. This is the most spiritual class I have attended. I love to hear Governor Abernethy lead his class, he is so spiritual. It is no wonder he has such a good class. May the Lord raise up many such leaders."

When one remembers that it was three miles from Mr. Fletcher's home to the city, over a rough and hilly road, and that he always walked, he will see something of the devotion that inspired this man of God in all his work. The leaders to whose classes he was welcomed often as their leader himself, Governor Abernethy and Mr. H. Patterson, were among the most thoroughly equipped leaders the writer has ever known. Both men of age and experience, well trained intellectually as well as spiritually, they were well adapted to the largest influence in their spheres.

Up to about this time Mr. Fletcher's official relation as class leader had been with classes in rural neighborhoods. In 1868 he was appointed by Rev. C. C. Stratton, pastor of Taylor Street Church in Portland, leader of the morning class. He had felt that God was preparing him for greater work, but what it might be he awaited God's movings to know. So when this appointment came it was accepted as from God, and he girded himself to meet its responsibilities in the best and most useful manner possible. That the reader may see a little deeper into his heart we quote from his journal under date of June 8th, 1869:—

"Brother Stratton appointed me to take charge of the Sabbath morning class at 9 o-clock. My confidence is strong in God that He will greatly bless me in my labor of love. I have been asking my Heavenly Father that He would open a door for me where I could be most useful for the remainder of my life, and I have reason to believe that He has work for me to do in Portland. O, may I have that grace in my heart that will make me to be greatly useful in winning souls to Christ. O, my Heavenly Father, when I think of a poor sinner, who could not even read, saved by grace and made to be holding such an important office in Thy Church, surely I must say, 'eye hath not seen nor ear heard, neither have entered into the heart of man the things which thou hast laid up for those that love thee.'"

Mr. Fletcher began his service in his class meeting with eight present. His first work was to hunt up the long-absent ones and gather them back into the fold. Meantime his relation to his former class

on the mountain some miles from the city continued, and they were as faithfully watched and
sought after as ever.   But the time was coming
near when much of that widely scattered work in
the country that he had attended to so carefully
for such a length of time would be given up to
other hands, and his own would be transferred to
the more concentrated field of the city.   After
some weeks of the usual routine of class meetings,
prayer meeting and Sabbath school work in and
about the city, and at the same time attending to
his temporal affairs in his usual exact and conscientious manner, the Quarterly Conference of
Taylor Street Church, under the advice of the
then pastor, Dr. J. H. Wythe, offered him the very
responsible and delicate place of janitor of the
church.

Taylor Street Church has been for many years
the leading church of Methodism in the Northwest. A large church, with a membership count-
ing many hundreds, and a great congregation, it
was no small work to care for the church itself and
look after the accommodation and comfort of the
congregations that thronged its services.

It is not strange that Mr. Fletcher hesitated.

It was unlike any other work to which he had ever been called. It had much to do with the temporal side of the church work, and might possibly interfere with the spiritual opportunities that were so dear to his heart. But to him opportunities were providences, and he must needs lay this before the Lord and ask for His direction before he answered. He says: "I spread the whole matter before the Lord and asked Him what I should do about it. The passage of Scripture that was applied to my mind was, "Behold, I have set before thee an open door." In this word God's voice was heard and accordingly he accepted the offer of the church, and immediately began to prepare for the removal of all his personal interests to Portland. He entered on the duties to which he had been called on the 8th day of November, 1868, with this characteristic prayer upon his lips:

"May God enable me to discharge all my duties in the most profitable manner, and may my coming among this people be abundantly blessed."

CHAPTER V.

JANITOR OF TAYLOR STREET CHURCH.

"I rest in Thy Almighty power;
The name of Jesus is my tower,
    That hides my life above.
Thou canst, Thou wilt my helper be;
My confidence is all in Thee,
    Thou faithful God of Love."

—Charles Wesley.

WITH the poetic quotation from Charles Wesley that stands at the head of this chapter, Mr. Fletcher entered upon the work of 1869. He had "entered the open door," and in the name of the Lord went forward to whatever might await him of duty or privilege in the years to come. As, in addition to that specific work that came to him as janitor of the church, the incessant watchfulness and care for the comfort of the congregation, the constant attention to all those matters that would make the public services attractive and profitable, he retained his relation to his classes as leader and performed his work among them with singular effectiveness and intelligence, this may be a proper place to give some description of the character of that work.

The place of class leader in the Methodist Episcopal Church has been hardly second to any other in its direct influence on the personal experience and character of the church itself. Its theory supposes that only such as are themselves well grounded in the Christian life shall be appointed to it. Besides this, there must needs be a discriminating if not profound knowledge of the vital doctrines of the Holy Scriptures, especially as set forth in the teachings of Methodism in her books of theology and in her standard hymnology; the most complete and perfect that is to be found in all the Christian church. Then, an essential facility in simple doctrinal statement and application, with a readiness in calling to mind suitable stanzas of a hymn when it can serve a useful purpose; a discriminating judgment of human nature; kindness coupled with firmness; a heart full of love and yet full of fidelity; a soul capable of feeling the burdens and temptations of others, and an ability to lead those of others to the great Burden Bearer and teach them how to "cast their cares on Him who careth for them;" all these and many more kindred qualities are essential to the successful class leader.

It will easily be seen that this is a combination of mental and moral and spiritual and even physical qualities that is not easy to find, and when it is found it is an inestimable treasure to the church that possesses it. It is not too much to say that the spiritual results of the work of the preacher in the pulpit are largely saved or lost to the church by the influence of capable and godly leaders, or by the neglect and weakness of incapable and careless ones. Many hearts are prepared for a tender and helpful waiting upon the teachings of the pulpit by the more direct and personal teaching of the leader before the pulpit speaks, or after it has spoken by the careful and loving application of the truth heard to the mind and heart of the hearer by the leader, whose alert mind and receptive heart have taken close grip of each truth needed by the individual members of his class.

William Carvosso has been the patron saint of the class-room in nearly all the life of Methodism.

If a Methodist needs to be told who William Carvosso was, his ignorance of Methodist lore is too dense to be illuminated by such a side reference as we are able to make to him in such a work as this. If any man has ever been appointed a class leader, and has not proceeded at once to familiarize himself with the doctrines and rules of the church he served, and in immediate connection therewith the personal lives and official methods of such men as Carvosso, that fact alone has doomed him to failure, and the souls of those committed to his care to injury and loss. No one acquainted with Mr. Fletcher could expect for a moment that he would not lay hold of all these helps, and also of any other that might come to his knowledge.

There were many things in common in the conditions, character and work of the two men. Both were born in low estate. Both entered upon life in humble callings. Both were entirely uneducated in their youth. Both learned to read and write when considerably advanced in life, and after the grace of God had touched and awakened their intellects to an ambition to do good in the world. Both had charge of several classes at the same time. Both kept up a wide and continued corres-

pondence with the members of their classes. Both
had great and evenly sustained zeal in their work.
Both had strong faith. The parallel might be continued. Something of this came doubtless from
the fact that Mr. Fletcher, the younger, was a
careful student of Carvosso, the elder, not as an
imitator, but as a disciple, intelligently compre-
hending principles and carefully applying them.

A few extracts from Mr. Fletcher's journal
touching his class methods and his personal experiences will give the reader a better knowledge
of the elements that combined in him to make his
work a success than a more extended ex parte description. Under date of January 24th, 1869, he
writes:—

"Sabbath morning. I read our church rules to my class
this morning. I want them to be well informed in the doctrines and principles of our church. It is a source of much
regret to me that our people are so ignorant in relation to
these. I intend, by the blessing of God, not only to build
my class up in the 'knowledge of the truth,' but also in their
duties as members of the church."

What pureness, what trueness, what faithfulness are manifested here! On the very next Sunday, Januay 31st, he makes this record:—

"In place of our regular class meeting this morning I had each member of the class select such a portion of one of our hymns as would best correspond with their present experiences. I had two objects in view in this. One was that they might be made more familiar with our hymns, and the other that I might vary the order of exercise to the greater interest and profit of the members. I wish I could get them to study our hymn book more, for I believe that, next to the Bible, it is the best book for us to study. It contains such a body of divinity, and such soul-stirring praises to God that its greater use would be a great benefit to them all. They would then 'sing with the Spirit and with the understanding also.' "

An experienced Christian can readily see the skill of "the master workman" displayed in such diversified and ingenious methods of spiritual work. He will imagine what an impression would be made on other minds when one would quote such stanzas as:—

"Now I have found the ground wherein
    Sure my soul's anchor may remain;
The wounds of Jesus, for my sin
    Before the world's foundation slain;
    Whose mercy shall unshaken stay
    When heaven and earth are fled away."

Or this from Charles Wesley:—

"Long my imprisoned spirit lay
  Fast bound in sin and nature's night;
Thine eye diffused a quickening ray;
  I woke, the dungeon flamed with light;
My chains fell off, my heart was free.
I rose, went forth, and followed Thee.

And then some weary one sings from Bonar:—

"I heard the voice of Jesus say;
  'Come unto me and rest;
Lay down, thou weary one, lay down
  Thy head upon my breast!'
I came to Jesus as I was,
  Weary and worn and sad;
I found in Him a resting place,
  And He hath made me glad."

And then some one further on in the divine life,
better acquainted with God than most, repeats as
the experience of perfect trust:—

"Thee will I love, my joy, my crown;
  Thee will I love, my Lord, my God;
Thee will I love, beneath Thy frown
  Or smile, Thy scepter or Thy rod.
What though my heart and flesh decay?
Thee shall I love in endless day."

Now it is a stanza expressive of penitence, now
of pardon, now of cleansing, of sanctification, now

of faith's triumph, now of the hope of heaven. Who could go away from such a service unedified and unblest?

Another marked peculiarity of Mr. Fletcher's work as class leader was the great interest he took in the new members, especially the young people, added to his class. Evidencing this is a record he makes in his journal under date of March 14th, 1869. He says: —

"Sabbath morning. The Lord Jesus has added one more new member to my class. This is a dear little boy, Herbert Northrup, who has early given his heart to Jesus. O, may I have grace to take care of these precious lambs which are entrusted to my care. The Lord is blessing my class. Many of them are truly hungering and thirsting after righteousness, and I am looking to see them filled."

Northrup was a name long and greatly honored in the Methodism of Portland, and of the entire Northwest. Herbert was the eldest son of E. J. Northrup, who was converted to God in the meetings held in Portland by Rev. A. B. Earle, to which reference has been previously made. The father lived a very devoted life, and, although engaged in large business enterprises, gave much time and means to the direct spiritual work of the church. He became the leading layman of the city, was a delegate from the Lay Electoral Conference of the Oregon Conference to the General Conference, and, when in the full course of his most useful life, was suddenly killed by an accident in his storehouse. He was, and, in a moment, "he was not, for God took him." Herbert, the young boy of whom Mr. Fletcher speaks above so tenderely, lived a few beautiful years after he united with the class of Mr. Fletcher, and then went to join his translated father in the celestial land. Their names have the perfume of ointment poured forth in the church in Portland.

We have already mentioned Mr. Fletcher's habit of a close and religious correspondence with members of his classes and others in whom he took a special interest, as one of his distinguishing qualities as a class leader and general Christian worker. This extended not only to those who were near, but to those far away as well. Wherever he journeyed, by sea or land, his heart never forgot the land of his birth, nor the friends of his early life there. His journal often speaks of some of them in terms of peculiar tenderness. While he was communicating to them assurances of his recollection of them, and often making to some of them remittances of money, he evidently never forgot their spiritual good, but wrote and prayed in constant hope that his words might become the instrument of their salvation. Nor was his labor in vain, or his hope in this regard cut off. An incident illustrating this is given in his journal February 22d. 1869. He writes of two friends in Ireland:—

"I received a letter from Eliza Floyd and Margaret Floyd which has made my heart glad. I find by it that God has seen fit to use me as the instrument in His hand in their conversion. O Lord, 'my cup runneth over' with joy to think that Thou canst convert even in Ireland as well as in Oregon. and that in every nation he that feareth Thee and worketh righteousness is accepted of Thee.' O may the good seed that has been planted in their hearts bring forth abundant fruit to the glory of my God. Although I am far away from them, my heart is often present with them, and they are doubly dear to me now that we are united in the bonds of Christian love. O may the riches of God's grace be multiplied to them, and may they become burning and shining lights in that portion of God's green earth. Although I am far away from it I love it still. My soul often desires that God in His good providence should open the way that I might once more visit them, and there make known to them personally the riches of His grace. But I will lay myself in His hands, with the assurance that, if it is His will, I shall go there, but if it is not, then His will, not mine, be done.

"In all my ways His hand I own."

The summer of 1869 marked a serious decline in
the spiritual condition of the church with which
Mr. Fletcher was connected. It seemed a period
when mere "table-serving" and temporalities occupied the minds of both pastor and people to a very
alarming extent. Mr. Fletcher was greatly dis-
tressed over this condition of things, and for a
time was inclined to believe that his work in Portland was done, and God was about to call him
into some other field; but, though he felt this
impression for a short time, opening providences
soon satisfied that there was yet work reserved in
the counsels of the Master for him to perform here
and he turned to it with unabated zeal, even when
so many about him had doubtful and fainting
hearts. Another class—a class of young boys—
was put under his care, and he gave it the same
faithful attention and prayerful instruction that
marked his relation with all his classes. He was
also elected a member of the Young Men's Christian Association of the city, and took an active
and useful part in all its work. About this time
there fell into his hands a copy of George Muller's
"Life of Trust," a work that records the wonderful
experiences of that man of God in entering on and

and carrying forward his great school and orphan-
age undertakings. The reading of this book was
a means of great benefit to him. as it has been to
thousands. From its reading he was led to adopt
Romans 13-8.: "Owe no man anything. but to
love one another; for he that loveth another has
fulfilled the law," as the rule for the remainder of
his life. At the close of 1869 he makes this remarkable record:

"I have not been absent from my class meeting nor from
any other meeting of the church a single time during the
year. I have spent over eleven hours every Sabbath in the
church attending to the various duties of the sanctuary.
and notwithstanding all this labor and care and anxiety.
God's grace has always been sufficient for me. On entering upon 1870 it is with the desire in my heart to be more
faithful. more useful. and more abundant in those labors
of love. I have set apart Friday of every week for the service of the Lord in any way His providence may direct."

Any one who has followed carefully the story of
Mr. Fletcher's life up to this time. must surely
wonder how he could be more faithful. except in
the use of the new strength he had been constantly
gaining in his life of singular consecration. up to
this hour.

About this time another class of twenty-four

young girls was committed to his care. This class had been under the instruction of Mrs. Patterson, a most capable and godly woman, whose personal influence over Mr. Fletcher himself had been a strong factor in the development of his own high Christian life. It was no slight mark of the high place he had attained in the confidence of the church that these places of special responsibility fell to him, not from any desire on his part to obtain them, but because no one else seemed so well fitted to aid the young people forward in the true divine life as he. Not only this, the young people themselves were delighted to have him as their counselor and friend, and under his direction many of them were early brought to a clear knowledge of their adoption into the family of God. With the care of three of the most important classes of the church, the diversified and never ceasing duties of his janitorship, and also his wide correspondence, it is not strange that at the close of the year he felt that his duties pressed heavily upon him. Yet he expresses "thankfulness that God gives them to him to discharge," and that he "has reason to belive that he blesses him therein." With such reflections on his work, and with such resolutions for the future, Mr. Fletcher comes to a point that marks the beginning of another distinct era in the story of his life.

CHAPTER VI.

MARRIAGE.

"We are weaving the thread of our life's webs
    Day by day;
And its colors are sometimes sombre,
    Sometimes gay;
For we dye it with every passing thought,
And by words and deeds is the pattern wrought."

—Bradt.

ON the 24th day of May, 1871, Mr. Fletcher was united in marriage with Miss Lizzie Brown. As some notice will hereafter be given of the relations of his companion to the larger and most useful part of his career, it is only necessary now to make such mention of her as seems to be needful in connection with the incident of their marriage. Mr. Fletcher himself was fully impressed with the belief that this marriage was of the Lord's own ordering, and he therefore entered upon it in a devout and tender frame of mind. Miss Brown was about his own age, and well calculated to sustain and help her husband in the work in which he was

now engaged, and in that upon which he afterwards entered.

Miss Brown was born in Buffalo, New York.
She was left an orphan at an early age, yet in early
childhood she gave her heart to the Lord, and
lived a pure Christian life through all the changes
of her subsequent career. She came to Portland
about a year before her marriage, and was a close
attendant on the services of the church. In this
way she commended herself to the confidence and
love of the church, and especially of Mr. Fletcher,
and both accepted it as of the Lord's will that they
should become one in Christ Jesus. Our readers
will hear more of her hereafter.

Mr. Fletcher always took great interest in his
pastor. In proportion as he was a man devoted to
God and able to instruct the people in the "things
pertaining to life and godliness," he found in Mr.
Fletcher a signal help in leading the people forward. But if the pastor chanced to have a worldly
spirit, or was disposed to compromise truth by
yielding to doubtful social customs or demands,
though no factious and contentious opposition
was made to him, yet he could not be in doubt as
to the position Mr. Fletcher occupied. He was

friendly and gracious with all, but his closest Christian intimacies were with those who walked on the highest paths of the Christian way. In reading his journal, the writer has observed that every one of his pastors was welcomed with words of trust and hope, even if thereafter he showed his want of the best instincts of the spiritual life, and led, or permitted his people to drift into doubtful ways of worldly compliance. In such case, and in these things, Mr. Fletcher parted company with him, even while he gave his active support in every way to the general work of the church. Several instances of this kind had occured previous to the time of which we are now writing, but in none of them was there the slightest evidence of disloyalty to the church, but constant tokens of the greatest fidelity to all her interests and economy. The work of the summer of 1871, was not closing prosperously with the church where he had labored so long and earnestly, and as conference approached he was excedingly anxious in relation to the appointment of a pastor for the next year. This did not arise out of any question of personal friendship, but with a single reference to the spiritual condition and progress of the church.

The annual conference of 1871 was held in Taylor Street Church, and Bishop Edmund S. Janes was its presiding officer. Our readers will remember that Bishop Janes had traveled in the stage coach from Yreka, California, to Oregon, in company with Mr. Fletcher in 1863. They recalled the incidents of the journey with mutual satisfaction as they met here eight years thereafter. When the conference closed Bishop Janes announced as the pastor for the coming year, Rev. G. W. Izer, who was transferred from the Central Pennsylvania Conference to the Oregon for this special charge. Probably no pastor that the church ever had influenced the thought and hope of Mr. Fletcher more strongly or more favorably than did Mr. Izer. Young, alert, spiritual and intellectual, his ministry was full of an attractive and stimulating unction that peculiarly attracted the people, and was especially helpful to Mr. Fletcher in his personal experience, as well as in his relations to the work of the Master that lay so near his heart. It is with no feeling of surprise that we read in his journal at the close of the conference session, "I look for great things from the hand of the Lord through him this year." At the end of the first

month of Mr. Izer's pastorate, the house was filled
with a very serious congregation; a number had
been converted, several had professed sanctification, the prayer meetings and class meetings had
revived and the entire outlook for the church had
been changed from one of clouds and doubt and
fear, to one of bright skies and conquering faith,
and confident courage. No wonder that Mr.
Fletcher greatly rejoiced, giving glory to God.

At this period in the life of Mr. Fletcher, we
note, for the first time, a record of his entering
upon a work that was eventually to prove the
great work of his life. What it was will appear if
we quote a sentence or two from his journal under
date of September 14th, 1871:

"Since Conference I have been distributing tracts among
the hotels and boarding houses and shops and steamboats,
and have done some little missionary work in connection
with it. The Lord blesses me in it, and my prayer is that
He will continue to make me more useful. I love this work
of distributing tracts; it gives me such opportunities to
speak a word for Jesus to the sailors about the ships and
inviting them to our meetings."

About two weeks later he records that:

"For the two weeks work twenty-four persons have been
converted and four made perfect in love, and among the

twenty-four are three sailors belonging to vessels in port. I trust the Lord has used me as an instrument for the salvation of these souls, and I look for still greater results yet in the salvation of more of them before our meeting closes."

Two weeks later a second record says that fifty-two had been converted and six made perfect in love, and that among them was another of the "sailor boys," the second mate of the English bark Bristolian, making three from her and one from another ship. He prays that the little leaven that has been hid in the heart of these sailor chaps will so work that the whole of the ship's company will be leavened."

The early occupation of Mr. Fletcher as a sailor even long before his conversion, now began to show its ffects in his readiness for the work God was preparing for him. He could not have imagined as he was passing through the hard lessons of a sailor's life what an influence these lessons would have after many years upon his career; and certainly those who saw him in his rough garb and perilous exposures would never have thought that out of these untoward conditions would come at last a character so refined and a life so conse-

crated. With a new attainment of strength, and
this leading by Providence into new and promising fields of Christian work, Mr. Fletcher closed
the year 1871. His reflections are so pertinent,
and express so much of the spirit that was his best
furnishing for the work of his life, that we give an
extract from them under date of January 1st,
1872:

"The past year has been one rich in mercy to me and my
companions. I have devoted this year entirely to the service of God in the various duties connected with my work
in the church. It has been the burden of my prayers to
God that He would so bless me in the labors of my hands
that I would be able to devote all my time and little talent
to Him, and to-day, in looking back over the year that is
just closed, surely my prayers have been most abundantly
answered. My Heavenly Father has has not only given me
a nice home, but one of the best of companions to share it
with me. We are one in spirit in serving the Lord. In entering this new year myself and wife have consecrated
ourselves and all that we possess anew to God, to be used
as His good providence may direct; and may the grace of
our Lord Jesus Christ abide with us."

This character of work continued with Mr.
Fletcher through 1872. The latter part of the
year was signalized by a gracious revival of religion in the church in Portland, and in the revival

Mr. Fletcher was in labors most abundant, and his soul flamed with purifying fire. Probably Taylor Street Church never had a higher and purer religious life than at this time.

Mr. Fletcher's work was extending more and more among the sailors. He says of January 1st, 1873:—

" I have been greatly blest in my labors among the sailors in this port. How thankful I am that I have been to sea myself in my younger days, as I can adapt myself so readily to their wants. I am so well acquainted with all the "land sharks" and sailor boarding house runners, that I am able to warn the sailors of their dangers when on shore. I have been very succesful in getting many of them to attend my Sabbath morning class, and many of them have been converted in the class rooms, and have gone to sea happy in the Lord. I have realized in the past year more than ever before the importance of living a holy life, and being fully consecrated to God and His work: as it removes from me a man-fearing spirit, and gives me that liberty in my work that I need so much. My wife is also rejoicing in the same blessed experience with me. It makes our work so pleasant for us, and our home so happy, and it gives us favor with the people so that we can do them good."

During 1873 the shipping entering the Port of Portland greatly increased, and so Mr. Fletcher's work among the sailors became more and more

important. A much larger number than ever
were induced by him to attend church and class
meeting, where he found it easy to teach them,
and lead them into a Christian life. So rapidly did
this work grow under the faithful hand of Mr.
Fletcher that on January 1st, 1874, we find him
expressing the expectation of seeing at no distant
day "a Seaman's Chaplain and Bethel for the men
of the sea."

CHAPTER VII.

CRUSADERS.

Not many lives, but only one have we
Our only one;
How sacred should that one life ever be!
That narrow span,
Day after day, filled up with blessed toil,
Hour after hour still bringing us new toil.

—Bonar.

EARLY in 1874 there occurred in the moral and religious history of the city of Portland a series of incidents with which Mr. Fletcher and his wife were actively identified, that should have some notice in this work. They grew out of the organization and work of "The Woman's Temperance Prayer League."

The saloon power had become so formidable in the city, and all the crimes that are fostered and sustained by that power so prevalent, that a number of the Godly women of the city, of various denominations, banded themselves together for a "crusade" against it. There were perhaps forty in all who enrolled themselves in the band; women who led the active religious work of the several city churches, and whose hearts were stirred within them when they saw the city so wholly given up to the ravages of intemperance and all its attendant crimes. They resolved to go upon the streets, and even into the saloons, and by songs and prayer and personal appeals, try to stay the tide of destruction. There were but thirteen of them at the first enrolment, and the second name on the list was "Lizzie Fletcher." They had a very active and and even enthusiastic support from Rev. G. W. Izer, pastor of the First M. E. Church; Rev. G. H. Atkinson, pastor of the First Congregational Church, and Rev. Mr. Medbury, of the First Baptist Church. The other pastors of the city gave the movement only a reluctant support. Their work was first confined to earnest prayer in the meetings of the League and at home, but before long they felt it their duty to go upon the streets and carry the battle of prayer to the very gates of the saloons. It was the veritable march of the "Crusaders" when these godly women went forth out of the front door of old Taylor Street Church, led by the unseen "Captain of their Salvation" against the giant foe of all good on the crowded streets of the city, not knowing to what insults and oppositions they went. Martyrdom itself could not be more to be dreaded. Foul insults of low and villainous speech were heaped upon them from the habitues of the saloons. Horsewhips were plied upon their backs. Streams of water from the hose pipes were turned over them, but none of these things moved them. They had hold of God, and nothing seemed able to make them unloose their grip. They reviled not again. They replied to angry oaths with sweet-voiced songs and earnest prayer. They remembered the Master's code of Christian warfare, "bless them that curse you, and pray for them that despitefully use you and persecute you." This they literally did. No braver, nobler Christian spirit ever was exhibited.

So deep was the impression made on the public mind of Portland by the heroic and devoted as well as determined course of these noble women— for they were noble in every sense—that the saloon forces saw that their cause was doomed to fall unless, in some way, the efforts of these women could be stopped. Five of the women were arrested for praying on the street, under the charge of disorderly and riotous conduct. Among these was Mrs. Fletcher. The city magistrate spent two days in the mockery of a trial, and then they were found "guilty" and fined "$5.00 each or one day in prison." They refused to pay the fine, choosing, properly, to endure the imprisonment rather than in any way to recognize the semblance of justice in the action of the court, and accordingly they were locked up in the city prison. Such is the mercy and justice that wrong gives to right when right makes even the insurrection of prayer against wrong. As though prisons could manacle prayer, or iron walls defeat the power of God to finally avenge His people!

At evening of the day of their incarceration Mr. Fletcher visited the prison where they were confined, to observe their spirit, and especially to see if his wife needed anything for her comfort during the night. He says:

"I shall never forget the impression that was made on my mind while there with her in prison for about half an hour before she was locked up for the night. She was very happy in the Lord; not only willing to spend one night in prison, but also to suffer death, if need be, for the cause of Christ. All the ladies that were with her in prison would have been willing to do the same."

How strange the senseless enthusiasm of sin for its own cause! How strange that eighteen centuries have not sufficed to teach iniquity that there is no real refuge for it in law; that its victories are always its defeat, and its crowns of thorns on the brow of right always change to coronets of glory.

Immediately after these ladies were released from their imprisonment they and their coadjutors of the praying band continued their work on the streets and in the saloons until June, but even besotted crime did not attempt to stay their proceedings by prosecutions or limit the freedom of prayer by prison walls.

Soon after the close of this active "Crusade," the pastoral term of Rev. G. W. Izer closed at Taylor Street Church, and he was transferred to the East. His preaching and pastoral labor had proved a great mental and spiritual help to Mr. Fletcher, and it was with sincere regret that he bade him "good-bye" as he retired. Nor had Mr. Izer any less cause to feel gratitude to Mr. Fletcher for the full, constant and efficient support received from him. In the cheering words, unpretending kindness and helpful attentions given him by the latter at all times and under all circumstances not a little of the good wrought by Mr. Izer in Portland had its origin and support.

The years 1875 and 1876 were, with Mr. Fletcher, in the main incidents of his life, like those that had preceeded them. There was no lessening, but rather an increase of his responsibility and work. The number of ships that entered the port continued to increase, and with that his work among the sailors enlarged. More of them attended his classes and the general services of the church than ever before. Evidently the seed that Mr. Fletcher almost alone had sown in the hearts of "the men of the sea," who had visited the port was beginning to bear its ripened fruit all over the world.

Many incidents of thrilling interest occurred in connection with his work: incidents that made his name and work familiar to seafaring men everywhere. At one time a sailor was converted in one of his meetings in Taylor Street Church. The next morning Mr. Fletcher met him and inquired if he had written the good news of his conversion to his wife in Liverpool. The sailor replied, "No; I could not keep her waiting for two weeks to know what God had done for me, but I have sent a cablegram this morning." So the good work of this true friend of the seamen was becoming known in every port. It may be truly said that, up to this time, very little had been done in Portland for the salvation of the sailors that was not done directly through the instrumentality of Mr. Fletcher. Of the increase of this great work we shall see more hereafter.

As we pass down the way in the story of Mr. Fletcher's life, it seems needful that we illustrate the influence that continually aided in the development of his life by some references from the men and women with whom he wrought in the intimacies of Christian friendship. Few men have had their friendships pitched on a higher key, and he had the faculty of absorbing good out of them all. His own sincerity of word and deed was so obvious that he needed no other credentials to open his way to the trust and confidence of others.

Among those who, for years, was most closely connected with him in his church work, and perhaps more intimately connected with the development of his own spiritual life, was Mr. George Abernethy. His death, which occurred on the 2d day of May, 1877, brought to the whole church sadness, and especially to the heart of Mr. Fletcher. When we study the character and career of Mr. Abernethy, and then consider how intimately these two men were associated in the work of the church in Portland for so many years, we shall understand this fact better.

Mr. Abernethy was a thoroughly trained and cultivated Christian gentleman. Few finer specimens of that beautiful product of the Christian civilization of America have been seen among us. He was eminent in all the relations of a most enterprising and useful life. After an early discipline and training in business and in Christian life in the city of New York, under such eminent teachers as Nathan Bangs, Samuel Merwin and their compeers and coadjutors, he was chosen by the Missionary Board of the M. E. Church to be put in charge of the financial inerests of its missions in Oregon in 1839, and came to this coast in the capacity of Missionary Steward. Here he served faithfully in that capacity as long as such an officer was needed, or until 1846, when he entered business for himself, and became the best known of the early merchants of Oregon. He was chosen as

Governor of the Territory under the Provisional Government, and re-elected to the same place, serving as such until the general government extended its jurisdiction over Oregon in 1848. He led the laity of Methodism in all good works for many years; and was the first lay delegate to the General Conference of the Methodist Episcopal Church from the Pacific Coast. When he died, not only did the church here feel the shock of a great loss, but the entire State of which he had been one of the most influential and discreet founders, paid its tribute of praise and gratitude at his tomb. With him as a brother beloved, Mr. Fletcher sustained a most intimate relation, and without doubt drew from his richly stored mind and ripe Christian experience much that was helpful to his own life and work. To have held such relations to such a man for so long a time was surely pledge enough of the personal character and religious worth of Mr. Fletcher.

For nine years Mr. Fletcher had served the church in the relations which have been traced in the preceeding pages. At the close of the ninth year he was granted a leave of absence for four weeks, for a visit to California. When this was done he makes in the journal the following remarkable statement regarding these years:

"I have never been absent from my class for one meeting since I came to this Church, nor from any of the church services. Since I became its sexton in 1868 to the present time, I have been enabled by the blessing of God to attend to all my various duties, having the best of health, and above all, the favor of God in my work. I believe that the Lord has appointed me to this work. When I took charge of the church as its sexton, I felt fully convinced in my own mind that this was the work which the Lord had for me to do, and now, as I look back, I can truly say that I was not disappointed. It may be my life work, so far as I know. The Lord's will not mine be done. I want to be where the Lord thinks best."

Such was the record Mr. Fletcher had made in these nine years, and such the spirit he had borne through them all. If it could but enter into the lives of all God's people what wonders of redemption would be wrought in the world! God's call was never unheard. Everything must wait for God's voice. That was the only determining factor of duty. Inclination was nothing—only God's will. Steadily as time moved onward he moved on and out to do God's will. And everything was done in love. Strength after strength was attained through duty done. All strength was used. He never frustrated the grace of God; never consumed it on his own desires. And so he came to a period and a fact in his work that marked the opening of a new era to him, and those who had been a chief object of his solicitude for many years, "the men of the sea."

CHAPTER VIII.

WORK WIDENING.

Wait cheerily, then, O mariners,
  For daylight and for land;
The breath of God is in your sail,
  Your rudder is His hand.

Sail on, sail on, deep freighted
  With blessings and with hopes;
The saints of old with shadowy hands
  Are pulling at your ropes.

Behind ye holy martyrs
  Uplift the palm and crown;
Before ye unborn ages send
  Their benedictions down.

Sail on! the morning cometh,
  The port ye yet shall win;
And all the bells of God shall ring
  The good ship bravely in!

—Whittier.

WE have now come to the opening of a work in the life of Mr. Fletcher for which, it seems to us, all that preceeded it was but a preparation. When we saw him a sailor on the deep, tossed by the waves and driven by the winds of all the seas, or stranded on many shores of many lands, he seemed but a sailor, destined, in all sure probability, to continue his adventurous voyages until, in some stormiest day, he should earn a sailors' heroic burial in the deep bed of the sea with the unnamed thousands of those, to all appearances like him, who have thus sailed and thus sunk into the unfathomed depths. But they were not like him, though they thus seemed. God had more for him than for them because he had more for God than they. When we saw him a miner, with pick and shovel bending over the rocky pits, or digging in the deep gulches of the mountains of California, or daring the granite fastnesses of Idaho for gold, he seemed only a miner; likely to beat his life out against the iron walls of the mines or lose it out of sight of men with the hundreds of thousands the engulfing mines have swallowed up forever. He seemed like them—they like him. But God had more for him than for them, because he had more for God than they. When we saw him in the ordinary pursuits of a laborer on the fir-clad hills of Oregon, or in the streets of the city, he seemed but the ordinary laborer, fated to the weary round of daily and nightly toil for bread,—only for bread—until that weary round ended in an unmarked grave; where ends the bootless struggle of more than half of the human race. But God had more for him than for them, because he had more for God than they. That more was a purpose; a looking forward, a making the most and the best of to-day as all he had, remembering that to-morrow was God's, and that he could only be ready for God's to-morrow by rightly using his own to-day. Thus he made the sailor's voyages and the miner's toil preparations for the greater, higher tomorrows that followed on his lower yesterdays.

The era in his life to which Mr. Fletcher had been thus conducted by God's gracious providence he had, in a divine way, foreseen and expected, and had been doing much to create. It was the formal and public inauguration of Christian work among "the men of the sea," who, in the courses of trade or the pursuits of adventure, were finding their way into the ports of Oregon, and especially into Portland, in great numbers. Our story of his life has repeatedly mentioned his personal attention to them and his earnest solicitation for their salvation. These seemed, as we recorded them, but casual incidents, quite aside from the main purpose and interest of his life, while, in reality, they were chief factors in the make-up of that life. He was marking out the most important and far-reaching labors of his whole history. The people of Portland, among whom he had gone so long, and to whom he was so well known, did not understand that his quiet and unostentatious visits to the wharves and the decks of the vessels lying at them; to the sailor's boarding houses, and to all the resorts where the sailor boys were enticed to their ruin, with his bundles of tracts in his hands, which he distributed as leaves of the tree of life to all, were putting in action a train of influences that meant a world-wide evangelization and would make Mr. Fletcher himself one of the most widely known of the religious workers of the coast. But so it was. It was, as ever, God taking care of His own, and taking pains that His watchmen did not wake in vain.

It is probable that the modern church has not begun to appreciate the evangelistic value of such work among the sailors; even if she has appreciated the sailor himself as a man. A converted sailor is a world-going missionary. No pent-up village or narrow country neighborhood confines his influence. From port to port, from country to country, from capital to capital, he is borne by the free winds of the sea. He knows all continents and all islands. He is a citizen of the world. He belongs to the demorcracy of humanity. He is God's free evangel; heaven's roving messenger of truth and love to every land and every clime. Thus the winds waft His story. Thus the waters roll it. Every ship that bears him becomes "the old ship of Zion," freighted with salvation and sailing to all ports. "The breath of God is in her sails, her rudder is His hands," as she sails on freighted with hope and salvation for the world.

Portland had grown to be such a seaport and to command such a commerce with foreign nations as awakened its great Christian merchants to the need of organizing a Bethel Home" and a "Mariner's Church" for the benefit of the hundreds of sea-faring men constantly in the city. Accordingly, on November 4th, 1877, union services, under the auspices of the leading churches of the city, were held in Taylor Street M. E. Church, for the purpose of making such an organization. Rev. R.

S. Stubbs, a very able and devoted as well as experienced minister, had been appointed by "The
American Seaman's Friend Society," of New York,
Chaplain for the port of Portland. Mr. Stubbs was
present, and his evident adaptation to so great a
work stirred the people to enthusiasm. Mr. Stubbs
had been a sailor for many years, and had risen to
the command of vessels, and, of course, understood the needs of sailors, and well knew how to
provide for their supply. The meeting completed
plans for work, raised over $5,000 for its com-
mencement, and had assurances from the best
sources of further aid as it would be required in the
progress of the work. These facts greatly encouraged Mr. Fletcher in the hope that his ruling desire would have a larger fulfillment in the salvation
of his beloved "men of the sea."

At this time one of the most eminent of pulpit
orators of his day, Doctor Guard, visited Portland,
delivering two lectures and one sermon. They
were greatly appreciated by all, and especially by
Mr. Fletcher. By a happy incident he introduced
a friend of his, Mr. John Wilson, a leading merchant of the city to the Doctor, who immediately
recognized him as one of the teachers of his **early**

boyhood, and greeted him with most loving remembrances.

Under date of January 1st, 1879, Mr. Fletcher writes:—

"There is a most remarkable work of grace now going on among the seamen in this port. Chaplain Stubbs is working faithfully on board the ships in port. My wife and myself have attended many of the night meetings on some of the ships during the last five weeks. I have not seen such a revival since I came to Portland as is now going on among the seamen. I think there must have been about forty seamen converted up to the present time. Truly, the little leaven that has been working for the last few years is now showing its power. I hope it will not stop until the crew of every ship in port shall be leavened of righteousness."

With the added work that came to Mr. Fletcher in the organization of the Seaman's Friend Society in Portland, there was little diminution of his work in the church itself as janitor and class leader. At the same time his reading and studying of the best class of Christian works increased. His journal often speaks of them with most appreciative language, especially of such as touched the practical and experimental sides of Christian life. For those that had tendencies opposite to the purest and highest experience he had no place. One, for which he had paid three dollars, under a mistaken idea of its character, he consigned to the flames, "so that it could do no harm." Still providence seemed directing him toward a wider opportunity for usefulness to his beloved "sailor boys," as the very best field for the use of his mature Christian powers and experience. Making up his mind after mature deliberation and prayer that the Lord had other work for him to do, in August, 1879, he resigned his place as janitor of Taylor Street Church. Of so much public interest was the event that the Pacific Christian Advocate, whose editor, Rev. Dr. Dillon, was at that time serving as pastor of the church Mr. Fletcher had so long served, gave this appreciative notice of it: —

"Brother Fletcher has been a fixture in the janitorship of Taylor-street church for ten years. If ever faithful and devoted labor was cheerfully and well performed it has been done by him; for all these years promptly at the time, without a failure, he has rung the bell for all the gatherings of the church, has had the church ready for occupancy, dusted, cleaned, ventilated and warmed: often in very cold weather sleeping at the church Saturday nights so as to start the fires in the furnace very early in the morning. Not only this, during all this time he has been present every Sunday morning at the 9 o'clock class of which he

is leader. But he is gone, and we fear "we ne'er shall see
his like again." We are only too glad to have him with us
yet in his pew, and in the class and prayer meeting, where
he will still be found upon every opportunity that he can
avail himself of."

These words of his pastor were but an indication
of the place Mr. Fletcher had won in the hearts of
all the church and congregation, the largest in
Portland. The care and punctuality with which he
had attended to his duties in Taylor Street Church
for so many years had attracted the attention of
the directors of the Portland High School, and
they sought his services in the like office in that in-
stitution. He accepted their proposition, as of the
Lord. His work threw him into close association
with hundreds of young people, and a very cultivated body of teachers, with all of whom he soon
became a favorite. His genial disposition, quiet
and obliging manner, and his careful consideration
of the comfort of all and the happiness of each not
only secured their confidence but won their affection, and he held their full esteem for all the years
that he served in that capacity.

With him one of the chief reasons for choosing
this position was that it gave him the week day

evenings and all of the Sabbath to pursue his work among the seamen. More and more his heart was drawn to this, and more clearly God's providence was opening it to him. With him opportunity was duty, and a chance to do was always earnestly improved. Accordingly he had no sooner entered his new field than we find him drawing nearer to "the men of the sea." Within two months of the time he began his work in the school he makes this characteristic entry in his journal:

Nov. 9th I got Dr. Nelson to consent to lead my morning class for the next three months so that I could have more time for work among the sailors on Sabbath morning. I visited four ships this morning, and distributed one hundred pages of tracts among the men forward. I also got five of the men to accompany me to church. O, may the Lord bless my work among these men of the sea.

Nov. 16—Sabbath morning. I had a good time in my visiting the ships, giving the tracts to the men, and in speaking to them of Jesus, who is always the sailor's friend. I told them his very first disciples were sailors, and that of all men sailors should be first to serve him. As I had spoken to the crew of one of the ships somewhat freely, I asked them how many of them would come with me to the church that morning to hear His word preached for themselves. Five of them came with me.

Nov. 23.—Only time to visit one ship this morning. After speaking to the men forward and distributing some tracts.

I went aft and spoke to the officers, gave them some tracts, and got the first and second officers to accompany me to the church.

This character of hand to hand and heart to heart work was pursued by Mr. Fletcher with the faithfulness and zeal of an apostle. Nearly every Sabbath morning he would be seen coming into Taylor Street Church with a company of "sailor boys" dressed in the garb of the sea, conducting them to eligible seats, sitting with them, watching intently the effect of the word upon them, ready to take advantage of all influences and impressions to lead them to Jesus.

In closing up his record for the year 1879 he gives—

A VISION OF THE BIBLE.
By a Seafaring Man.

"As I lay musing a vision passed before me of a noble ship. She was built in New Jerusalem, and her builder and maker was God. Her timbers were of the strong oaks of Zion, her masts of the tree of Calvary, and her rigging of the cords of love. Her sails were the doctrines of salvation, her cable a three-fold cord of faith, hope and charity, which could not be easily broken. Her helm glittered like the star of prophecy, her anchor was of gold from Immanuel's Land; her crest was the emblem of righteousness and her name was "The Word of God." From stem to stern, from keel to deck she was a goodly ship. Her deck was a broad platform on which Christians of all denominations might stand. Her guns thundered forth the terrors of the law, but her mission was emphatically peace. Her weapons were not carnal but mighty through God to the pulling down of strongholds. Her painting was beauty; she was streaked with light and sprinkled with blood. Her crew were the Apostles and Prophets, her passengers true believers, her captain the Prince of Peace. Her cargo was Truth, and her broad banner bore the inscription "Glory to God in the Highest: Peace on earth, good will to men." She was sailing over a tempestuous sea. The billows of error drove furiously against her bows, but her bulwarks were impregnable. She sailed from the port of heaven and her destination was to all the habitable parts of the earth, and her mission to the ends of it. The nations hailed her approach with joy. She scattered blessings in her course, and returned homeward bound freighted with living souls and cast her anchor in the haven of life under the throne of God and of the Lamb."

With this "vision" Mr. Fletcher closes his record of the year 1879. During it his words and his life among the seamen had brought help and encouragement to many a burdened heart, and hope to many a despairing breast. His cheerful presence, his light-like smile always stirred to better thoughts and higher ambitions all those with whom he mingled, and the memory of them sailed in the minds of hundreds of sailors on every sea. Whenever the sailor's thoughts would turn toward Portland, "Father Fletcher," was in his mind's eye; and to very many of them already it was his tender countenance, his vigilant guardianship, his Christian counsel awaiting him on the Portland docks that constituted the strongest desire to again return to rest for a little on the peaceful bosom of the Oregon port.

CHAPTER IX.

BROADENING LIFE.

Through seas more vast than these of earth,
 Blown straight by heavenly wind,
They sail with freight of precious worth,
 These merchantmen of mind.

In alien zones, through sun and cloud,
 With varied cargoes fraught,
What intercourse and traffic crowd
 The argosies of thought.

O, happy they who walk the strand
 Whereon those billows roll,
Whose ports, by right divine, command
 The commerce of the soul."

       —Clarence Urmy.

FROM the closing date of the last chapter for five years Mr. Fletcher continued the identical character of work described there. He had charge of one of the most important classes of Taylor Street Church, and led its members forward in the cultivation of the graces of the spirit with the same care and success as attended his work among the seamen. Members committeed to his care by the successive pastors of the church under whom he served, were never neglected or forgotten, and very few, if, indeed, any of those put under his guidance ever strayed from the ways of well doing. "By their fruits ye shall know them," is an eternal principle of judgment as to character and life. Judged by this test Mr. Fletcher's life had rare perfection. Its influence over others was always, even uniquely, pure. It had in it a living principle or germ of growth, and so it spread its fructifying sap through every fibre and vesicle of the souls it touched. Souls born into the Kingdom by his fatherhood carried a vigorous life in them from the very hour of their birth. Parenthood germinally conditions sonship, spiritually as well as physically. To be well begotten and well bred is to inherit character and quality and power. "Blood will tell." By the application of these principles to the life of converts the character of those by whom they were begotten in the Gospel is clearly defined. In the case of those among whom Mr. Fletcher's work was mostly done during this time there was need of a vigorous inborn life to carry them through the comparatively stormy conditions of their early Christian life. Out on the wild seas, almost before they have lived a single day in the consciousness of their new life of faith, visiting distant ports, surrounded by rollicking, roaring mobs of sin-intoxicated men; mocked at, ridiculed, opposed—if the life in them was not strong and forceful at the very beginning it were no great wonder if they did not endure. For these and other reasons which will appear hereafter, we see the uniqueness of the work of Mr. Fletcher, as well as the exalted qualities of the spiritual nature that he put into it. He so impressed himself and his own spiritual life upon those with whom and for whom he labored that, as a presence invisible to others, and yet visible to them, he walked the streets of the city, rode on the waves of the sea, sat in the pews in the church, joined in the songs of the sanctuary with those children of his begetting and love wherever they were. In this respect, in a finite way and with a few, he was with them to the end of the world, as Christ in an infinite way, and with all that knew him, pledged that he would be "always."

It is in this way that good lives are perpetuated;

given an immortality outside of themselves. One said "the evil that men do lives after them, but the good is often interred with their bones." This saying can hardly be accepted in its broadest sense. It is because good once done does not die, but "lives" after he who did it has gone back to dust, that good makes any gain over evil. "The eternal years of God" belong to good and truth, while "the death that never dies" is the doom of evil and falsehood. This is the vital motive to goodness of action and purity of life. "The righteous shall be in everlasting remembrance, but the memory of the wicked shall rot." So the memory of this friend and servant of the humblest occupant of the forecastle on the poorest ship that came to the port where he labored so long and faithfully will be green with verdure of immortality when the very name of the proudest captain that ever sailed the seas, whose life was evil and wicked, shall rot out of all mention by men or angels. God keeps the records of the book of lives, and He never forgets.

"Father Taylor" once described the career of a young man who came from the country to the city, who fell into one temptation after another till he became a degraded castaway. When he seemed

to have reached the lowest depth of horror, Father
Taylor, with a look and tone that chilled the very
marrow of the bones of those that heard him,
cried: "Hush! Shut the windows of Heaven.
He's cursing his mother!" He would, if possible,
keep the horrid degradation of this boy, who had
thus desecrated the holiest name on earth and thus
defiled himself, from the eye of the recording angel.
So goodness does not seek to perpetuate the memory of wickedness, but rather to blot it out. But
it does seek to perpetuate, to keep alive, the remembrances of the righteous.

In connection with his work among the seamen
and also in the church during the five years from
1879 to the opening of 1886, Mr. Fletcher continued as janitor of the Portland High School, where
several hundred of the brightest young people in
the city shared his attentions and enjoyed his
friendship. He won their confidence and so they became his friends, and in no small measure their love
of him widened all his subsequent opportunity for
doing good, and in no slight degree accounts for
the very remarkable hold he secured on the confidence of the best citizens of Portland. But the
time was nearing for which providence had been

preparing him, when he was to withdraw from some of the fields in which he had wrought so long, and devote all his time to the benefit of the seamen.

About the first of January, 1886, Chaplain R. S. Stubbs was transferred by the Seaman's Friend Society from the charge of the Bethel work in Portland to the superintendence of the work of that society on Puget Sound. On his retirement Mr. Fletcher was left in charge of that work in Portland. This brought him to the conclusion to which providence had long been pointing, that this was to be his one field of ultimate toil. Accordingly we find this entry in his journal at this time:

Jan. 1.—I intend, when my school year closes, if it be the Lord's will, to enter entirely upon the Bethel and ship work in behalf of the "men of the sea," and make it my life-work, and try to save these dear men in Jesus; for I know by sad experience of my own how terrible are their besetments, while they are in port.

Jan. 3.—This Sabbath I visited the ship Carmarthen Castle and met with the steward who was converted when he was here eight years ago in the ship Robert Lee, and also four more converted men in the ship with him. I had a most precious season with them.

Jan. 21.—I was visiting some of the ships this morning down at the Mersey docks. The sailors had just come on board half drunk, as they had been on a spree all night, and were quarreling with each other, as I was standing on the dock debating in my mind whether I should go on board just at that time or not, I asked the Lord what I had best do. The blessed Holy Spirit applied the words to my heart that God spoke to Moses: "Now, therefore, go, and I will be with thy mouth, and teach thee what thou shalt say." Exodus iv., 12. I said. "It is enough, Lord," and I just stepped aboard and met the captain on the poop. After shaking hands with him, he said, "See, there is a specimen of our British sailors," pointing to his men. I told him that his men would be all right but for the cursed whiskey that was in them; that that was the cause of all the trouble with his men. I told him that I would just step down into the waist of the ship and see what I could do to break up the row among them. He said: "You had better not go among them," but I said: "I have no fears at all"; so I stepped down to where they were wrangling. As one of them saw me coming towards them he came to meet me. I took him by the hand and said to him: ᴉ am sorry to see you men at loggerheads this morning. But I can sympathize with you for I have been in the same way more than once myself, and I know just how you feel." Just then another of them came to hear what I was saying, another one went and spoke to another, and one or two went forward, so the whole thing broke up, and there was no fight. I then went forward and said: "Men, I am sorry to see you in the way you are this morning. but I am thankful you are not in the lock-up, but on board of your own ship." I talked a little while with them, gave them some reading and left them. I then went aft and said to the captain,

"Blessed are the peacemakers." "Well," said he, "you had more courage than I have to go down among those fellows in the condition they were in." I then left him and went on board the ship Dovenby, and had a very profitable conversation with Captain Steele and his wife. So ended my morning's work on the ships."

Thus, Sunday by Sunday, year following year, did Mr. Fletcher find his way from deck to deck with his messages of "peace" and his invitations to Christ to officer and sailor alike. Sincerely humble, yet never shrinking from duty, full of a calm courage, yet never boasting of his bravery, this man of God constantly went forth to serve God by helping and saving lost humanity. Is there any other way of serving Him?

In April of this year Mr. Fletcher was put in charge of the Bethel work by the Portland Seaman's Friend Society, at its annual meeting. Since the removal of Chaplain Stubbs there had been no preaching in the Bethel, and Mr. Fletcher entered upon that field under discouraging conditions. In his usual way, however, he gave himself into God's hands for guidance and help in the broader field into which His providence had brought him, seeking the "Blessed Spirit's" aid in all he did. It seemed a propitious fact that this enlarged responsibility came to him when he was amidst the tender memories attending the 26th anniversary of his own conversion, and the 19th anniversary of his experience of perfect love. It is not strange that he says, in referring to this fact, as Isaiah said so long before him, "O Lord, I will praise Thee, for though thou wast angry with me, thine anger is turned away and thou comfortest me. Behold, God is my salvation, I will trust and not be afraid, for the Lord Jehovah is my strength and my song; He also is become my salvation."

With this evident call to the consecration of all his time and powers to the work of the seamen came the necessary duty of surrendering other work, which, however important in itself, and however pleasant to him it might be, would nevertheless occupy a large portion of his time. So in the early summer he surrendered his place in connection with the High School of the city, and, as it will give the reader a clear insight into his motives of life and rules of conduct in all that he was or did, his reflections on the occasion are given.

Under date of July 1st, 1886, he says:—

"I have resigned my positon as janitor of Park-street High School, which I have held for the last seven years, to enter more fully upon the Bethel and ship work. When I entered upon my school work seven years ago, I entered it as the Lord's work, and looking back now I can truly say it was of the Lord's appointment. I have been blessed both in spiritual and temporal things. The Lord has given me favor with both teachers and pupils, and also with the directors. I have never had an unkind word spoken to me during these seven years by any one connected with the school. I always kept the Lord and His work before me, and as I went in and out before them from day to day, I tried to set before them the example of a godly life both by my walk and conversation. O, I have enjoyed so many precious prayers for my teachers and pupils. I always felt it was the Lord's work I was doing, and now, as I give up my stewardship to Him who gave it to me, I ask Him to bless the seed that I have tried to sow in the hearts of these dear teachers and children during my seven years work with them.

"When I entered my school work, I received a salary of fifty-five dollars a month. The second year they gave me sixty, the third year seventy, and after that seventy-five dollars, so I can say the Lord has greatly blessed me in the labor of my hands. It seemed a great grief to the teachers and children that I should leave them.

"I had been enabled to build me a new two-story house on my lot on which I live, costing me $2,400, and is now bringing me $36 per month rent, and have left a balance of $800 in my bank account up to date. I can surely say that "goodness and mercy have followed me all the days of my life.' The Lord has brought me now to the place I have been working up to, so that I could give myself entirely to the work of the Bethel and the ships."

In this extract the reader will be able to see some of the elements of character that made the life of Mr. Fletcher such an eminently useful one in the sphere in which he moved. Stability of purpose, patient industry, unswerving fidelity, devoted piety, wrought out in the life of this once careless and godless sailor boy such a history of good deeds and noble works as really few have ever had recorded to their credit in the book of destiny. Feeling the call of God within him to devote himself to the benefit of that class of men amongst whom his own early life had been cast, he followed the openings God's providence made with the carefulness of a hunter on the track of game, never losing his purpose and never relaxing his effort until now he sees the desire of his heart accomplished and he is ready to fully enter into the call of his gracious Lord. If his erstwhile companions before the mast will carefully study this life and imitate it in the measure of their opportunity, how many a noble man will spring from the hard places of such service to the high and blessed places of such power for good as was his.

CHAPTER X.

WORK AMONG SEAMEN.

"And men who work can only work for men;
And not to work in vain, must comprehend
    Humanity, and work humanely,
And raise men's bodies still by raising souls
    As God did first."

RELIEVED now from the burden of his school work, Mr. Fletcher was at liberty to devote himself to his work in the Bethel service. He had hoped that a chaplain who was a minister would have arrived before he entered fully upon it, but as his coming was delayed and the demand was so urgent, and so many sailors seemed waiting for some one to guide them in the right way, that he could but enter the open door in the name of the Lord. So on the evening of Sabbath, July 4th, he began "Gospel meetings" in the chapel of the Mariner's Home. A large congregation was present, and one sailor was converted. On the following Sabbath night another large congregation met him again at the same place, and two were converted to God. During the week he followed this result up by visitations and prayer with the sailors in their rooms, and on the following Sunday evening his faithfulness was rewarded with two more conversions. The same character of work with the same result of weekly conversions continued for many weeks. It is not likely that any popular pulpit in Portland gathered such a harvest of souls for the Master during this summer month of July as did this worker among the sailors in the "Mariner's Home."

On the 22d of August Mr. Fletcher records a service held for him by Rev. T. L. Sails, at that time a very evangelical and successful minister in the Oregon Conference of the M. E. Church. Mr. Sails had been a sailor, and reached Portland some years before as such, "having no hope and without God in the world." He chanced to fall into Taylor Street Church one evening when revival services were being conducted by its pastor, Rev. G. W. Izer, and was led to seek God at its altar. It was not long before he was converted, and soon after his natural gifts of speech and his evident consecration commended him to the church as called of God to the Gospel ministry. He was licensed as a preacher, and entering the ministry of Oregon, for about ten years he fulfilled it with a fervency and zeal that gave promise of far more than average usfulness and success in his calling. When in the culminating vigor of his work he sickened and died, having vindicated his Christian character by the authority of a spotless life and most heroic ministerial service. Having been a sailor in his youth, and being skilled in the vocabulary of the seas, and with a warm, sympathetic heart, and genial and bounding spirits, he was admirably adapted to the work among the seamen. Many thought, and among them Mr. Fletcher, that he should enter that work.

His visit at this time to the Bethel was a marked event. He was among his brethren of the sea. He knew a sailor's heart. He understood their temptations. He sympathized with their weaknesses. He pitied like the Master. And having traveled the way himself, he knew well how to guide a repentant sailor's soul to God. "Brother Sails was perfectly at home among my sailors, and let himself out," writes Mr. Fletcher. "He had great freedom in speaking and was assisted by the blessed Holy Spirit himself, which carried the truth home to the hearts and consciences of all these wanderers from God. We had a glorious meeting. He spoke on the "Prodigal Son," of which there were many present."

From July to about the first of September Mr. Fletcher had full charge of the Bethel work in Portland. At this latter date Rev. Mr. Gilpin, of England, arrived as Chaplain. The period during which Mr. Fletcher had charge of the work in the Bethel was marked by more conversions and a deeper spirituality than any other of its history. During the five months, besides his three weekly public services in the chapel, and his visits to and care over the sailors when they were on land, he made 148 visits to ships in port and conversed with their officers and crews, distributed 6000 pages of tracts and other reading matter. He also visited a large number of families in the interests of his Bethel work. Twenty-eight sailors were converted and he gave fourteen Bibles to those converted who had none. This is a record of work and success of which any pastor might well be proud.

Mr. Fletcher, in his usual grateful way, gives "all the praise and glory of this blessed work to the Holy Spirit," who so obviously attended and sanctified all his services. And yet the human basis of it all was in Mr. Fletcher's own adaptation to the work in which he was engaged. His naturally broad humanness, his plain, unstudied common sense, his kindly interest in every one that needed help, his calm fearlessness, coupled with a real humility, were the constitutional personal elements that adapted him to his work. Then there was another fact, well stated by himself in his journal, when accounting for the failure of a chaplain, that at the same time accounted largely for his own success. He says:—

"It takes a man who has been to sea himself, and has lived in a ship's forecastle and has gone through its trials and hardships. It is only such a man who can fully enter into the sympathies of these dear men of the sea. I feel thankful to God that I had spent my younger days on the sea, and had such an experience that the Lord is now enabling me to use it to call these dear men of the sea out of darkness into His marvelous light."

In the course of his visitations to the large number of ships that lay in the harbor during the present season, Mr. Fletcher found a large number of

Christian captains, as well as many seamen who were truly devoted laborers for the Master. On the 8th day of January, 1888, he records the fact that Captain Lloyd, of the bark Dora Ann, preached at night at the Bethel with excellent effect. The congregation were mostly sailors. It seemed to point out to him the approach of the time when "the abundance of the sea shall be converted to God," and the very ships of commerce should become flying evangels carrying to every land the "glad tidings of great joy" to all people.

Not far from the Mariner's Bethel the Portland corps of the Salvation Army had, at this time, its barracks. Many sailors attended these meetings, and many of them were converted. Mr. Fletcher wrought in harmony with them, often attending their services, giving them much aid in their work. While he was receiving encouragement and help from them, and with the broad Christian charity that always distinguished him, extending to them all the encouragement in his power, Chaplain Gilpin, who had charge under the Seaman's Friend Society, of the Bethel work in the port, took a violent stand against them. This fact greatly embarrassed the work of that society, and while Mr.

Fletcher's personal influence remained unimpaired among the sea-going people of the port, kept the seamen away from the Bethel services. But ship visitation was continued by him with equal and even increased diligence and effectiveness, and with no diminution of results. A few extracts from his daily record will show his faithfulness in this work, as it will also some of the results of the same method of work in other years.

"Jan. 27, 1888.—I spent the forenoon in visiting six ships at the Albina docks, and had a profitable talk with the officers and men, some of whom are to leave on their way to their home ports today and tomorrow. May the Lord keep them on their way."

"Feb. 2.—Visited six ships. I met one of the men of the four-masted ship Ben Dauran, who was here eight years ago when we had a great revival among the ships in port. He knew me as quick as he saw me, and we found that as "iron sharpeneth iron, so a man sharpeneth the countenance of his friend." One of the men of the bark Peebles-shire, who was converted at the Salvation Army meetings, and left for home in his ship this evening, promised to write me on his arrival there. May the Lord give him a prosperous voyage, and make him abundantly useful in bringing his shipmates to Christ."

"Feb. 15.—Visited six ships this afternoon and held conversations with both officers and men. I had a long talk with Mr. Mortimer, the first officer of the ship Cimara. He is a good Christian man, and is much liked by his crew. He was converted here in our ship meetings some eight years ago, and is much interested in our Bethel work, but feel that we cannot succeed in it without a change in our chaplain."

"Feb. 16.—This afternoon I visited two ships and had one of the best times I have enjoyed in talking to the first officer and carpenter of the bark Kier. They wanted me to give them an account of my conversion. The Holy Spirit gave me words to speak to them, and I hope and trust the same Holy Spirit carried it to their hearts and consciences to the saving of their souls. I have been asking the blessed Holy Spirit for some time that he would teach me how to perform my duty in the best possible manner among my brethren of the sea. I want Him to fill me with His unction, to enable me to speak with power to the hearts and consciences of these sailors. I can truly say that he is answering my prayer, for He is giving me more liberty in speaking and praying in the last few weeks than I have ever enjoyed before.'

Thus from day to day and from month to month, year after year, Mr. Fletcher went his unwearied way of good doing, and thus the sailors that went out of the port of Portland over all seas and to all parts of the world bore the memory of this good man in their hearts, while the fruits of his toil for them ripened in their lives of devotion in every land.

The writer does not intimate that all this good

was the entirely independent result of Mr. Fletcher's work. He had many sympathetic helpers; many who loved him, prayed for him, encouraged him; but he gathered into his own life the impulse of their devotion and friendship and gave it out again to others, enriched, enlarged, sanctified, and mighty for larger good. Among those who occupied this situation to him was Dr. Samuel Nelson. Alike in many of their qualities, but unlike in others, they were knit together in a friendship and trust like that of David and Jonathan. Their Christian experience was of the same type; deep, steady, and well expressed in the phrase, "perfect love." The writer has known few if any in all his life who more nearly demonstrated a practical and constant fulfillment of the Saviour's summation of the perfect law of God: "Thou shalt love the Lord thy God with all thy heart, and with all thy mind, and with all thy soul and with all thy strength and thy neighbor as thyself," than in the lives of these two men. Charitable, tender-hearted, pure in thought and speech, gentle as sanctified womanhood, yet stable as the strongest manhood, they walked before the Lord and before the world with open and uplifted countenances continually.

On the 1st day of February, 1888, Dr. Nelson was translated. On the 3d his funeral was held in Grace Church, of which he, as well as Mr. Fletcher was a member. It would not be proper to omit, in this record, the tender reference to this event, and to the character of this dear friend in the journal of Mr. Fletcher for that day:

"I attended to-day the funeral services of that dear old saint of God, Dr. Samuel Nelson. Dr. H. K. Hines delivered a most affectionate and touching tribute to his memory. My own heart responded to every word he said of him, for I knew the inner life of Dr. Nelson better than any other member of the church. He was a lover of the doctrine of holiness, and knew the power of its blessed experience as well as myself. I first met the doctor in 1865 at the Ames Chapel camp meeting. I formed his friendship then, and as the years went by our love for each other increased. I always found him a brother beloved in the Lord."

They two, with a number of others connected with the most practical Christian work in the city, and who also enjoyed the most exalted Christian experience, walked in closest personal communion for many years. Often they sung what was but a reflection of their constant sentiment towards each other:—

"Blest be the tie that binds
Our hearts in Christian love:
The fellowship of kindred minds
Is like to that above."

In reading the record of Mr. Fletcher's work
from day to day as it is given in his journal, one is
greatly impressed with his sustained faith and enthusiasm in it. It lacked all the contagious inspiration that comes out of crowded assemblies, vocal
with music and thrilling with eloquent discourse,
with all the accessories of public worship, but was
simply the quiet, unobserved, hand to hand struggle of a single man, full of faith and love, with
other single men without either faith or love, in a
desperate endeavor to win these other men to the
"like precious faith" and the like "perfect love"
that filled his own heart. No braver, truer work is
ever done than that. The preacher in the pulpit is
helped and uplifted by the magnetic eye-flash of
approving or applauding hearers. He is in the
warm, comfortable shurch, shut away from the
storm, and shut away from the sight of human deg-
radations for the time, in what, both in surroundings and society, "is almost heaven." But one like
Mr. Fletcher threads dark alleys alone, buttons his

plain overcoat about him to break off the cold blast, walks icy decks, goes down into dark forecastles, looks on human degradation in its darkest deeps, grasps the filthy hand of the most fallen sinner, listens to the bacchanalian revels of the drunken and profane instead of the sweet, pure voices of the church orchestra, all to save those lost; all to rescue those fallen. Surely the Christ must needs be incarnate again in the very purpose of His first incarnation in such a man or he could not and would not do such work.

During the month of March in this year, 1888, he records the visiting of forty-six ships and conversing with officers and sailors, distributing religious literature, magazines, and current secular papers, and, in addition, made four visits to the hospitals of the city, and kept up his attendance on his class and prayer meetings in the church of which he was a member.

It will be recalled that Mr. Fletcher was laboring under the general direction of the "Portland Seaman's Friend Society." On the second day of May its annual meeting was held in the parlors of Ladd & Tilton's bank, and was presided over by Mr. James Steel, a prominent business man and a leading member of the First Congregational Church of Portland, and one of the steadfast friends of the work of Mr. Fletcher among the seamen. A synopsis of the report of work done by him during the year just past will very clearly indicate its extent and value. He says:

"Since my last annual report I have made 408 visits to ships in port, and had many profitable conversations with officers and men and apprentice boys. I have attended twenty-two ship's services with our chaplain, and have made thirty visits to the hospitals and enjoyed many precious seasons in speaking and praying with a great number of the patients in their several wards. I have written many letters to the men and boys at the different ports to which they sailed from here, and have received many encouraging letters from them. I have also received a large number of letters from the mothers of many of these dear boys, inquiring about them. I find this is becoming a very important part of my work. I have distributed thousands of pages of choice reading matter on the ships, for which all are very grateful. I wish especially in their behalf, to thank the many kind friends who have furnished me so much of this literature. I have often visited our "Seaman's Home" and conversed with its inmates, and tried to advance the Bethel and ship work by all means in my power. The officers and men and apprentice boys have always treated me kindly, and much good has been apparently done among them."

CHAPTER XI.

ON SHIP AND ON SHORE.

"If you cannot, on the ocean. sail among the swiftest fleet,
Rocking on the highest billow, laughing at the storm you
    meet,
You can stand among the sailors anchored yet within the
    bay,
You can lend a hand to help them as they launch their
    boats away."

                        —Phillips.

IT has been observed by the reader that for some time the work of the Chaplain of the Bethel had not been prosperous. The incumbent had high ideas of personal dignity, with a somewhat exalted churchism, and felt that it was his place to command and the sailors place to obey, even in matters of religion. He could not understand that Jack on shore was a freeman, and the very fact that

he had been compelled to submit to a vigorous discipline on the ship made him the more certain to
assert his independence when on the land. He was
then on an independent cruise, and he rather delighted in running close by the most dangerous
reefs, if only to show his own skill in avoiding shipwreck. He could be touched, but not by cold and
high-headed dignity. He did not care for a clerical
garb. He resented sing-song cant. Bustling rit-
uals meant nothing to him. He was not looking
for men of that ilk at all. In fact, he was not looking for anybody. Least of all was he on the hunt
for a man shut up in stone walls, sitting in a high
pulpit, and in a solemn air waiting for some rollicking tar to come in and bow down and say: "Most
Reverend Sir, won't you please condescend to tell
me how I may be saved?" Such a man, sitting in
"the dim—very dim—religious light" of such a
place is not very likely to have many "mourners'
at his "bench;" certainly not many of the gallant
and light hearted boys of the sea. The wonder is
not that they do not come, but that he sits there
and expects them to come. The free street, the
wide open door, the generous invitation going
straight to the heart, the manly recognition of the

sailor-boy's own manhood, the tender reference to his far-away mother, or the watching, waiting sweetheart, anxious for her absent lover's good, and praying for his safe return, these and such thoughts as these will gain his ear and hold his heart. When he learns to love the representative of Christ he will soon love the Christ he represents. There is no other avenue to the sailor's heart.

Unfortunately the Chaplain at this time in the Bethel had never learned this lesson. A good man undoubtedly, he was stern and inflexible. He was a bit of the rock of Horeb that by some accident had been dislocated and fallen upon the blood-bathed, love-illumined summits of the mount of the Cross and of the Transfiguration. He was the everlasting thunder of the law, jarring its discords of wrath amidst the heavenly symphonies of "grace and truth."

Mr. Fletcher, while doing the things of the law, always sang and talked and lived according to the strains of the "New Song," "Peace on earth, good will to men." This difference in feeling and its resultant expression in action, brought to him much trial, and, what was infinitely worse, greatly retarded the general work of the society. The ser-

vices at the Bethel under the direction of the
Chaplain were nearly deserted, notwithstanding the
work of Mr. Fletcher on ship-board and elsewhere
among the sailors was prosecuted with his usual
diligence and success. He did all he could to
remedy the evil by the most hearty assistance he
could render at the Bethel, and with some good results, but not so marked as he desired. By some
solicitation he succeeded in persuading the Chaplain to go out on the streets for a short service of
song before the hour for chapel services, and by
this means gather a larger number inside to listen
to the sermon which followed. Still even this
seemed not strong enough to overcome the evil
influence that paralyzed the public work at the
Bethel. It is no wonder that Mr. Fletcher earnestly prayed that "the Lord would send a change
soon in the Chaplaincy of the Bethel."

On the 12th of May he notes one of the peculiarly sad class of incidents that are always occurring
in seaports. The carpenter of the bark Clynder,
while endeavoring to cross a railroad trestle on his
way to his ship, while under the influence of liquor,
fell from it and was killed. His name was Jacob
Bremner, of Hamburg, Germany. Only a few days

before Mr. Fletcher had visited the ship on his
Sabbath morning round, and spent a half hour in
talking to the men in the forecastle, and distributing books and papers among them. This man was
doubtless among those who shared the loving min-
istrations of this lover of men at that time. It was
doubtless the last call of that kind he ever listened
to. It is not wonderful that the one who was God's
messenger in uttering that call should say, "I am
more than ever impressed with the necessity of my
work among these dear men of the sea, and that
what I have to do for them must be done quickly.
This makes the seventeenth that we have laid away
in our new mariner's cemetery since it was opened."
Sad as is that last record, there is a very glad one
that stands against it, namely, that many times that
number had come to this port "dead in trespass and
in sins" but had sailed away again with a new spiritual life in their hearts. While the sad hearts of the
friends of those who sleep in that cemetery will
turn towards Portland and think of their dead who
slumber there, many more will turn towards it and
think of their living who were born there unto the
new and incorruptible life. While the first will
think of Mr. Fletcher as the one whose hands

gently smoothed the dying pillow of wandering
sons or brothers or lovers, and whose care gave
them Christian sepulchre under the distant skies of
Oregon, the latter will think of him as the priest
ministrant at the altar of divine consecration when
their sons or brothers or lovers were "born into the
Kingdom of God." Or, they themselves, thus and
here born into that divine life, will turn back to it
in ever-recurring remembrance of the natal hour
and natal spot that will forever monument their
spiritual birth. They will sing:—

> "There is a spot to me more dear
>   Than native vale or mountain;
> A spot for which affection's tear
>   Springs grateful from its fountain."
> 'Tis not where kindred souls abound,
>   Though that were almost heaven;
> But where I first my Saviour found
>   And felt my sins forgiven
>
> O, blessed hour! O, hallowed spot
>   Where love divine first found me!
> Wherever falls my distant lot,
>   My heart still lingers round thee.
> And when from earth I rise and soar
>   Up to my home in heaven,
> Down will I cast my eyes once more
>   Where I was first forgiven."

And to many a one that spot will be the beautiful port of the Willamette, and the gentle pilot, who led the inquiring soul into the haven of rest and life will bear the name of Fletcher; and they "will glorify God in him."

Early in June of this year the receipt of a letter from a young man who had been a member some years before of the Sabbath morning class of Mr. Fletcher in Taylor Street Church, brought many pleasant and grateful memories to his mind which he thus records:

"I received a letter to-day from Brother E. R. Zimmerman, now of the Kansas Conference, and stationed at Reamsville, Kansas. This dear brother was put into my class by Rev. C. C. Stratton, our pastor, when he was converted. It was Brother Stratton also who appointed me leader of that class. While Brother Zimmerman was a member of my class he received the blessings of perfect love, and felt himself called to preach the gospel. So he went to the theological seminary in Boston for three years. After he got through with his studies he entered the Kansas conference, where he has been a good and faithful minister ever since. I had not heard from him for some years and my heart rejoices at the good news from him In looking over my old class-books from 1869 to 1880, I find that there are now five members of that Sabbath morning class preaching the gospel, and one died a few months ago. The first was Brother Zimmerman, then came

T. L. Sails, then S. O. Royal and A. J. McNamee, and later
E. A. Shoreland and J. C. Teter, the last two now in Africa
under that dear man of God, Bishop Taylor."

This quotation from Mr. Fletcher's journal is
given specially to show how the small seeds of
grace sown in human hearts, under the silent influences of pious culture, spring up and bring forth
their great harvests of goodness over all the world.
In this little class-room, under the guidance of this
unpretentious leader, these young men were being
trained in the most essential culture of a successful
career, a deep, profound religious experience. T.
L. Sails, a sailor rescued from his wide-world rovings by his conversion in Taylor Street Church, became one of the best beloved and most successful
of Oregon pastors, and then went up to his rest.
Stanley O. Royal is at this writing among the honored and useful members of the Cincinnati Conference. After some years of most devoted missionary toil under Bishop Taylor in Africa, E. A.
Shoreland stepped into the ascending chariot on
the banks of the Congo. J. E. Teter wrought no-
bly for the Master under the same great leader-
ship in the "Darkest Africa," when he returned to
another field in Florida. Not one of them but

bore some impress of the moulding spirit of Mr. Fletcher into all their splendid life-work. Surely "the children of the kingdom are the good seed," not so much by what they say and teach, as by what they are and do.

Only a month after the entry in Mr. Fletcher's journal made in relation to E. A. Shoreland, he chronicles the news of his death. Mr. Fletcher had so much to do with the first religious life of Mr. Shoreland that it appears proper to make some larger reference to him, and to the noble place he was filling even in his early manhood, in the work of the Master.

Shoreland was an English sailor, and came to Portland as such, and, like the great mass of sailors who came to this port at that time, wild and reckless. He had a strong, forceful, passionate nature; just such as must pour itself out either in good or evil. Here he left his ship and resolved to try his fortunes on the land, at least for a time. He soon found employment in such work as an uneducated sailor might do. His contact with men on the shore in the active business of life gave a new bent to his thoughts, and it was not long before his mind began to grasp the idea that there was some-

thing better in the world for men to do than to con-
sume the strong forces of mind and body in dissipa-
tion and revel, if not in crime. His powers of observation were keen, and he soon came to the conclusion that the moral help and the intellectual
stimulus he needed to make a man of himself could
only be had in the associations and fellowship of the
church. With full consecrations he began a religious life. His mental ambition was born with his
new spiritual birth. When his soul touched saving
grace his mind ignited at contact with "the mind
of Christ." So he became "altogether" Christian.
Soon he was licensed as a preacher, and labored in
an energetic though humble way in the chapels
and missions in and about the city. Laboring
earnestly during the week at such toil as came to
him, on the Sabbaths and in the evenings he
wrought in the spiritual and intellectual quarries
to save souls and to gain knowledge. He succeeded in both. It was not long until the door of
the Annual Conference opened to him and he took
his place in the line of the approved and improving
young pastorate of the church. Souls everywhere
were his hire in the fields of his labor. His sturdy,
well-knit frame seemed fitted to the heaviest bur-

dens of a rugged pioneer itinerancy. The church in Oregon began to count on him as one whose work would pillar her future with strength and beauty.

Just at this time the work of Bishop Taylor in Africa was drawing the vision of the church thitherward with a strange enchantment. Shoreland's was a soul to feel the contagion of Taylor's enthusiasm and consecration. He was **brave** enough to respond to it, and he entered the work in that dark land with an enthusiasm and a judgment that put him far towards the front of the workers there. But on March 31, 1888, his strong body succumbed to the burning grip of the African fever, and at Lorando he surrendered his purified soul to God and passed into the heavens.

When the intelligence of his death reached Oregon it awakened great sympathy in the heart of the church. The present writer, who was at that time editor of the Pacific Christian Advocate in Portland, and who had been Mr. Shoreland's pastor in the years of his early Christian life, gave the following notice of the event in his paper of July 12, 1888:—

"So this dear brother has given his life for Africa. He gave it really when he went there, for no one can go on such a mission as that without giving his life to it. The whole for life or death is determined when the work is undertaken. So it was with Brother Shoreland. Only a few minutes before he stepped on board the cars that bore him away from this city on his mission to Africa, we bade him adieu. Tears were in his eyes and ours, as we looked the last look of love, spoke the last word of fellowship. We have borne him on our heart daily since that hour. We resign that strong and consecrated manhood to death reluctantly, if we dare say that, and yet feeling that someway his going to Africa and dying there is a part of the price of Africa's redemption, and so our regrets are mingled with rejoicing at his entrance into the life eternal. Sails and Shoreland! How they loved each other; and how they have met so soon."

Mr. Fletcher's reference to Shoreland, when he received the intelligence of his death, was characteristically tender. He says:

"I have seen by the Advocate to-day the news of the death of our dear Brother Shoreland, who went out with Bishop Taylor under the call of God to help redeem Africa. Well do I remember when I first met him years ago with other English sailor lads, who had left their ships on this coast, wild and reckless, just as I myself used to be before the grace and spirit of God found me, as it afterwards found Brother Shoreland. Now he is gone to heaven to meet our beloved shipmate, T. L. Sails, who has just gone before him. I am still left to sow a little more seed of the kingdom, and, if possible, to save a few more of these dear sailor lads, so they too may become like these who have gone above, mighty through God in the saving of their fellows. May God fill me with grace and power for this great work

CHAPTER XII.

CORRESPONDENCE.

"It is a great mistake to think of converting the world without the help of the sailor. You might as well think of melting a mountain of ice with a moonbeam, or of heating an oven with snowballs; but get the sailor converted, and he is off from one port to another as if you had put spurs to lightning."

—Taylor.

DURING the summer months the ships that trade with Portland are mostly on their voyages out, and they do not generally begin to arrive in port for cargo until autumn. Consequently during these months there is little "ship work" unless "a wanderer" chances along. Much correspondence was generally carried on by Mr. Fletcher at this time with captains and sailors from their home ports. It was almost entirely with those who owed him some special gratitude for his care over them religiously when they were here, or from those who by his influence had been led to Christ

and had gone away Christians, even though they
came condemned sinners. Not infrequently the
friends, as mother, sister, brother or father of some
poor wanderer who had been sick and perhaps
died here, and had been tenderly watched over by
Mr. and Mrs. Fletcher while living or lovingly laid
away to rest when dead, would send some tender
and pathetic acknowledgment of that care and love.
A brief chapter of this correspondence, selected
from a few of the many letters received by them at
different times and on various occasions, cannot
but be interesting and profitable to the readers of
these pages; as they will show the high esteem
in which these lovers of their race were personally
held by those whom they so heartily and generous-
ly comforted and aided when they were strangers
in a strange land. Besides they will give some
glimpses of the trying life of the sailor and of the
terrible moral strain that is upon him to lead him
away from all good and truth and virtue, against
which the efforts of such men and women as Mr.
and Mrs. Fletcher, are about the only safeguard
and protection. They will be introduced without
any special chronological order, as they are used
only for the ends named above. The first is from a

lady of Birkenhead, England, in a full, round beautiful chirography, and is signed by "Kate Maclean," and is as follows:

"Dear Mrs. Fletcher:—My brother Hughie has told us so much about you and Mr. Fletcher, that we all feel as if we knew you; and we all feel so very grateful to you for all the kindness you showed him during his stay in Portland, Oregon. He did so enjoy being with you, and said it always gave him a taste of home when he went to your house. * * * * We shall always think of you with feelings of love and gratitude for all your goodness to Hughie."

It is suitable that this letter from the loving sister should be followed by one from the sailor brother over whose welfare she so tenderly watched. It was also dated at Birkenhead, April 23, 1890; and reads as follows:

"Dear Mr. Fletcher:—I suppose you have quite given up all hope of ever hearing from me again. I feel quite ashamed of myself for not writing you sooner, after all the kindness received by me from you and Mrs. Fletcher, which was so much more to me as I was in a strange place and so far from home.

"I have been working on board the ship for the past fortnight, so that will be in part excuse for not writing. We sail tomorrow for Sydney, New South Wales, with part of the cargo for Newcastle. I have often thought of the many happy evenings I spent in Grace Chapel, and how homelike it felt to get among kind people, and I feel quite sure that if the congregation knew how happy they make boys feel when in a strange land, and far from their friends, by their shake of the hand, it would pay them ten-fold. I suppose you are quite at home in your new church by this time, and I hope it pleases everybody, but if I ever go to Portland again I think I would feel more at home by going to the nice little chapel than to the new church.

"My father and sisters all wish to be kindly remembered to you and Mrs. Fletcher for your kindness to me; and I close with love and best wishes to you both from us all.

"Yours sincerely,

"HUGHIE MACLEAN."

What a beautiful glympse of real human brotherhood and sisterhood is opened to the mind of the reader in these two letters. The sailor-boy, swimming over distant seas on the rolling ship; the loving sister in the cottage-home following him day by day over the wide main with her heart's best love and her faith's most ardent prayers; the true, human-hearted Christian standing on the dock, half way round the world, awaiting, with wide open and protecting arms, the sailor coming from the seas; the little chapel out of whose doors and windows streams the inviting light of the Gospel; the congregation of loving worshipers extending their hands in glad greeting to the sea-worn sailor from another clime to the strong brotherhood and the loving sisterhood of the church; these are all a part of the beautiful whole of the scene these letters paint to the mind. Surely such facts and such work go far to prove that, even if humanity was all lost in Adam, it was all regained in Christ.

A sailor-boy who has been cared for and instructed by Mr. Fletcher and his wife while in port is now about to sail away on his long voyage. His vessel had dropped down the Columbia to Astoria, and just before she put to sea he wrote Mr. Fletcher the following letter:

"Dear Brother in the Lord:— I thought it good to write a line before we leave for home. We thank God for the visits which you have paid to us from time to time since we arrived in Portland. It is to be hoped that we will see the fruits of them some day if not now. We thank you for the reading which you gave us, especially for the book of sermons. It is singular but it is the very thing that I desired, so I consider the Lord sent it. Blessed ever be His holy name for His kind care of me. This is like the Lord in all His dealings with me. He supplies all of my wants and takes all of my cares. I did intend to visit you before I left, but you see the Lord sent what I wanted. I hope that your mission room will soon open. You cannot know what a comfort it is to have a place to go to where we may find

Christian fellowship with those who love the Lord and love to speak of these things. In my case you are the only one I have had a word with since I came there. I never neglected to try to lead any who were around me in the ship in the right, and had good hopes that all was well with some of them, but having no place where I could direct them when they might meet with what they needed to keep them from temptation they seem all to have fallen away. I think more of this as I see the need of their finding some kind friend who has influence to keep them from the "runners" and "boarding house masters." One of our men especially I will mention. He has a wife and little one at home. He had remained firm until the last day or two, when, through drink, he fell away and left. Here is a wife and little one left to get their bread as best they can, as the half-pay that she had stopped. I am sure if proper influence had been brought to bear on him the boarding-masters would not have got him.

"The papers and books that you gave will be read and distributed around on the ship.

Yours, in Christ,

WILLIAM BUNTING."

Member Seaman's Christian Life Boat Crew. Motto—"He that winneth souls is wise."

This letter indicates one class of perils to which the sailor in port is always exposed. Mr. Fletcher himself, in his early life, when on the sea had suffered from them, and he was the better prepared to guard those who came under his influence from them. There are always in every port land pirates who lie in wait to make Jack their prey. False, immoral, treacherous men, yea, and women too, whose sole business is entrapping the unwary into their dens of infamy and then robbing them of whatever they may have of worth, and then casting them out into the street, careless whether they live or die. Many and many were the sailor-boys Mr. Fletcher guided away from these haunts of death—these chambers of hell. He led them to the church. He took them to his own home. He was brother, father, protector to them. Mrs. Fletcher was sister, mother, friend to them. No wonder the sisters, mothers and fathers of these sailor-boys all over the world love and revere the names of these two angels of help to their brothers and sons in Portland. The Christ himself will say unto them, "inasmuch as ye have done it unto the least of these, ye have done it unto Me."

Some of these letters show something of the hard and harsh treatment given the sailors on board some of the ships. In a letter bearing date at Liverpool, from David Jones, we find the following:—-

"I arrived here Monday night, and we laid six days in Queenstown. The ship I came home on, (the Edward

O'Brien,) I need hardly tell you, was a very hot one; but I am pleased to say that I got along better than I did in any other ship. I have the chance of going back, either as third mate or second boatswain, but I would not go in her for $100 a month and have to beat men the way the officers did. There were four men in that ship triced up by the thumbs for threatening to kill the mate. One of them had a revolver in his breast at the time he was hanging up on the line; but he had no chance to use it, I suppose.

We had a very stormy passage. Two men were washed overboard, but we got them again with a great deal of trouble, more dead than alive. Another seaman fell from the rigging while reefing the sails, and broke his leg and cut his face."

This letter from David Jones was followed not long after by one dated Liverpool, August 26th, 1889, from Mr. E. Jones, the father of David, which has great interest as indicating the excellent influence of Mr. Fletcher over the life and destiny of these sailor-boys in all respects. The letter of Mr. Jones, Senior, says:

"Dear Mr. Fletcher: I now take the pleasure of writing you, hoping these few lines will find you in good health. David received your kind letter, which I think he answered the same week after receiving it. We were very pleased to have him home, also to see him looking so well. We scarcely knew him when he came, he has altered so much, but were pleased to see such a change in him for the better.

He is settling down better than we thought he would, and looks at things in a more sensible light than he formerly did. And, above all, we were pleased to see that he is a total abstainer. He was telling us he had not touched drink since he left the Arethusa, and we have no fear now of his falling away again. Many thanks for the kindly influence you have had on him, and the interest you have taken in his welfare. We assure you we have appreciated your kindness very much, although we can return you but poor thanks by letter. His mind seems settled on America, especially the district you reside in.

Well, he has left us once more. He did not go back on the Edward O'Brien. As there was very cruel treatment on board during her passage here, we did not wish him to go in her again. He sailed from Liverpool on the 12th of August on the Loch Broom, for Calcutta, and intends shipping from there to 'Frisco if he can. We hope he will soon meet with a ship from there. As he seems to have his mind on America, we think he would do better to settle ashore. With kind regards to Mrs. Fletcher.

Sincerely yours,

E. JONES."

One cannot read such letters without feeling that it is really easy to do good. A kind, sympathizing heart, good common sense, an earnest spirit and a soul in fellowship with the soul of Christ can hardly avoid doing good. It does not need great professions or even great abilities, only sincerity, truth and love. They were the elements that bore the mastery in the life of Mr. Fletcher, and that found for him so ready an opening into the hearts of sailor-boys with whom he came into contact. How many they lifted from profanity to prayer, from drunkenness to devotion, from revelry to reverence, from a life of aimless folly to a life of high and holy purpose, only eternity will disclose. It is the conviction of the writer that many a man who has stood in the high places of the church on earth may be found far below him in the preferments of the Church Triumphant. God does not forget, nor the Recording Angel keep the book incorrectly. If "patient continuance in well doing," if constant "looking for glory and honor and immortality" gives any assurance of "eternal life," or gives an advanced grade of heavenly reward, surely he will shine among the brightest "stars in the firmament forever and ever."

One other letter written by a young man of evidently more than average intelligence, must close this chapter of correspondence. It was written on board the English ship "Clan McPherson," in San Francisco harbor, January 11, 1891, and is as follows:

"Dear Mr. Fletcher:—Just a few lines to inform you of
our safe arrival here, for which I humbly thank God, for
only He knows how near we were to death on this
passage. We arrived here last Wednesday after a very
quick but a most terrible and disastrous voyage. We
experienced nothing but gales of wind the whole way; in
fact we have never had a dry deck until the day we arrived
here. The worst hurricane we encountered was on Christmas eve. Without exaggeration the sea ran mountains
high, and caused a tremendous amount of damage, and unfortunately some accidents, one of which nearly proved
fatal. This was in the case of an apprentice of the name
of Killam. The poor boy was knocked down by a large sea
and nearly drowned, so that it took us nearly two hours to
bring him to consciousness. He was horribly cut and
bruised about the head and on the body, so that we all
despaired of his life; but I am glad to say he is now recov-
ering. The same sea threw the ship on her beam ends and
the cargo shifting we remained in that dangerous predica-
met throughout the gale. Every wave that broke over us
that dreadful night threatened to swamp us, and every
minute we thought she would founder. We had a miserable
Christmas, Mr. Fletcher, as we were in the hold trimming
cargo all the time, with nothing for our Christmas cheer
but rum and biscuit, as nothing could be cooked in the
galley. Our two boats on the house were washed away,
the pigs and the pigsty, the posts along our bulwarks, and
everything that was movable on our decks. In fact, we
were a complete wreck. How grateful we are to God for
His goodness to us in enabling us to reach our destination,
I will leave you to imagine.

"Remember me to dear Mrs. Fletcher, and tell her again how grateful I am for her kindness to me while in Portland. I remain your sincerely attached young friend.

"G. J. SPINK."

What a picture of the perils of a sailor's life is here presented, not in the fancy paintings of a Marryatt or a Reid, but in the experience of this young sailor, who had this hard wrestle with the winds and the waves on this awful Christmas day. Surely these "sailor-lads," as Mr. Fletcher so often and so tenderly calls them, deserve the kindliest treatment of those for whose comfort and pleasure they "go down to the sea in ships and do business in great waters." Brave? The warrior before the cannon's mouth is not braver! When "the sea shall give up the dead that is in it," many and many will rise from their coral beds and seaweed shrouds to wear the whitest robes and bear the brightest crowns in Paradise.

CHAPTER XIII.

"Cast thy bread upon the waters, for thou shall find it after many days."— Bible.

TOWARDS the last of August, of 1888, the first vessel of the autumn merchant fleet arrived in Portland, and Mr. Fletcher hastened to greet its sailors with his usual messages of good. The summer had been spent largely in work in the mission Sunday school, and, as opportunity offered in services on the street and in the Bethel. But the prospects of the work in the Bethel were still clouded by the unfortunate condition of its chaplaincy. This, of course, was a sore trial to the patience and Christian forbearance of Mr. Fletcher, but he bore it with courage, and labored on to build up the general work, and to reach and save the individual seamen. He notes that at one of the Bethel prayer meetings a young sailor who had just arrived in port introduced himself and inquired if he recognized him, and when informed that he did not, replied, "Well, I know you. I was here eight years ago, when I was a boy, and you held meetings on our ship, the "Robert Lee." At that time the captain of the ship and four of the men were converted, this boy among them, and he still remained steadfast and gave good promise of a useful life among his shipmates. Thus the bread cast literally upon the waters was found again "after many days."

Early in September of this year the annual merchant fleet began to arrive in port and for the three following months Mr. Fletcher was kept busy in visiting these vessels, and, as he had opportunity, doing good of every kind to all on board. The cabin-boy and the apprentice was no more overlooked in these efforts than were the officers. He had the foresight to understand that the cabin-boy of to-day will be the master of to-morrow, and that a child saved to-day meant a man or woman prepared for the work of the Master after a time. So he let no opportunity pass to impress the young mind aright. And it must be said that there have been very few within the scope of the writer's acquaintance who have been as successful in this

work as W. S. Fletcher. Guileless and open hearted himself, low-voiced and tender in his speech, and
with a face lit up with the holy contentment and
satisfaction of his pure spirit, it was easy for him to
win the love of the young to himself, and then to
transfer that love over to the Master whose servant
and lover he was. His journal is full of references
to "picture cards," "lesson papers," &c., that were
left in the hands of the children on board the ships,
on the streets and in the Bethel Sabbath-school.
Especially as a ship was about to put to sea he
would appear on its decks with bundles of papers,
pictures, books, magazines, for all on board.
Many a heart was made glad at this thoughtful-
ness, and one can easily imagine the pleasure and
profit these contributions brought to cabin and
forecastle alike during the weary months of the
long voyages to the ports of the nether world.

In the midst of this most interesting work Mr.
Moody entered upon evangelistic services in Portland. Mr. Fletcher entered most heartily into
that work, and while he did not neglect his ship
work nor his general care for the sailors, he found
time to be present at many of the afternoon and
neary all of the evening services of the great evan-

gelist. He was not only present, he was an active
worker in the cause, and not a few souls were converted by his instrumentality during the meetings.
He records one conversion that occurred during
the meetings that, on some accounts, was worthy
to be recorded among the really wonderful triumphs of divine grace that are sometimes seen in
the progress of the Christian religion. It was the
case of a man of national fame as a lawyer and
a statesman, who had reached the age of probably
fifty-five years, and whose position and influence
was second to those of no man on the Pacific
Coast, Hon. George H. Williams. Mr. Williams
had been a citizen of Portland for thirty-five years.
For many years he had been the leading legal authority in the state, both as a judge upon the
bench and a practicing attorney in the courts.
For six years he had been United States Senator
from Oregon. For four years he had been Attorney General of the United States in the cabinet of
General Grant. He was a member of the Joint
High Commission that settled the Alabama claims.
He was the author of some of the most important
and useful of the reconstruction acts under which
the states lately in rebellion resumed their places in

the National Union. He was nominated by General Grant for Chief Justice of the United States after the death of Chief Justice Chase. Intellectually he was the peer of the great statesmen of that day of great men. But up to this time, the latter part of December, 1888, he "had never bowed his knee in prayer," though he was a man of high moral character.

The reflections of his own mind had been bringing him nearer and nearer to the faith of the Gospel, and the unsatisfactory character of mere worldly success had pressed itself more and more upon his heart as he had gone higher and higher in public standing and worldly fame. Mr. Moody's meetings were the occasion of bringing his mental convictions to the crisis of public action.

On the night of December 21. Mr. Williams stood up publicly, before a congregation of not less than 3,000 people in the "Tabernacle," and announced his convictions in clear and unmistakable words. He recited the movements of his mind as he was coming to the final conclusion intellectually, as well as the character of his action in finding his way, from darkness to light and from the power of Satan unto God;" and how, at last, that very day, in Mr. Moody's room, when the evangelist was opening to his mind the Scriptures and kneeling with him in prayer, God sent peace into his soul, and for the first time in his life he was made to understand what it means to have the spirit of God bear witness with his spirit that he was a child of God.

The effect of the conversion of Judge Williams was wonderful. His great, logical intellect, his high personal character, his almost world-wide fame, everything in his great history conspired to make this the most notable conversion that ever occurred on this coast.

In his plain, straight-forward remarks made on this occasion of his public avowal of conversion to the faith of Christ, Mr. Williams took occasion to say that he had been brought to his present step by careful study and long observation, and that it was not a sudden impulse or supernatural impression that led him to this public action, but a sense of duty and of fidelity to his profoundest convictions. It was a giving up to God worthy of such a man; and from that hour the position and action of Judge Williams on all questions of Christian service and life has been that of a true and humble follower of the "meek Nazarene." Mr. Fletcher, who was present on the occasion, speaks of it as "one of thrilling interest."

It is well that we close up the record of Mr. Fletcher's work for 1889. and give the beginning of it for 1890, in the words of his own journal:

"Dec. 31.—Mr. Moody closed up his mission here with a watch night meeting at the tabernacle. It was one of great power. The Tabernacle was packed from seven o'clock to midnight. The most of the city pastors gave short addresses. and Judge Williams gave a most thrilling account of his experience. Eternity alone can tell the good that has been accomplished by these meetings. I have been greatly profited by them. In the inquiry room I have spoken to and prayed with seventeen. Some of them were backsliders. some seekers, and some doubters. As the result of my speaking and praying with them five have professed to be converted. and two reclaimed from back sliding. and my own soul has been greatly blest.

I have written to Dr. Stitt, the secretary of the "American Seaman's Friend Society," and also visited two ships to-day. In looking over my work for the year that has just closed. my heart has been made sad at the little that has been accomplished in our Bethel work. It has been impossible to get the sailors or the longshoremen and their families to attend, the Chaplain's ways are so arrogant and domineering. Over two years ago we had a good congregation in the Bethel, both of sailors and longshoremen and their families, and a good supply of faithful workers, but now they are all gone.I do feel thankful to God that my way has not been hedged up in my ship work. My Heavenly Father gives me favor with both officers and men so I can do them good. That work has been greatly blest both to my own soul and my brethren of the sea, and the bread that before had been cast upon the waters has been found after many days. To God be all the glory."

Although Mr. Fletcher's work received the general support of the master's of the ships in which he labored, yet occasionally one was found who did not enter into his plans. On Sunday, December 6th, he refers to an incident that illustrates this. He says:—

"I visited one ship this morning and had a very profitable conversation with Captain Vaile on my spiritual work among the sailors. He is one of those men that believe it is all labor lost to try to do good to sailors. I think that I fully convinced him that so far as my own work is concerned, at least, I had led some of them to Christ and to a better life. I then gave him some of my own experience when I went to sea and was knocking around myself, and how the devil always used to keep to windward of me, but when I gave my heart to God then I got windward of him, and by the power of the blessed Holy Spirit I was able to keep him ever after under my lee. I then went forward and spoke to the men and boys and spent about an half hour with them with much profit to them and to myself.

"The way of the wicked is as darkness. They
know not at what they stumble." This is as true
in regard to the opinions of wicked men as in regard to their actions. The things of the Spirit are
only spiritually discerned. Blinded hearts make
blinded eyes. Men who themselves have not
learned to "walk by faith," nor realized in what
mysterious ways God can work and does work in
saving men, reason but to error on such a theme.
It is not strange, nor does it necessarily imply any
unusual perversity, that such opinions are held and
expressed by such men. One like Mr. Fletcher,
whose own feet had been taken out of the mire and
the clay of wickedness, and had been put upon a
rock, with his goings established in righteousness
and true holiness, knows that grace is omnipresent
to save the lowest and most degraded, and so he
labors on rescuing the lost, lifting up the fallen,
turning many to righteousness who "shall shine as
the stars forever and ever." But for such workers
our whole humanity would sink to fathomless
depths of degradation. It is only such that go
down to the lower stratas of social life, on which
really all above depends, and raise the whole by
purifying and elevating the foundations. We can-

not be too thankful for them, nor too grateful to
them. Illustrating this, on the 26th of February
he makes the record that "I had three of the sailors
of the ship M. E. Watson to spend the evening at
our house. Had also Miss Nellie Viggers with us.
We had some good singing and spent a most pleasant time, and closed with some refreshments that
wife got ready for us and a precious season of
prayer. The boys left for their ship, which lay at
the Albina dock, very much pleased with their
visit."

After such an evening and with the sacred home-
feeling that it must needs have inspired in their
hearts, these boys would walk safely for a while
amidst any temptations. Only those who never
tried these holy experiments of love on the hearts
and lives of others doubt their efficacy to save even
the wayward and the prodigal. It is when they are
out in the cold world of consuming sin, with no
Christly hand stretched out to their help, and no
welcoming home-door opening to the cheering fellowship of home-love that these men fall such easy
victims to the evils that allure with the false promises and counterfeit seeming of that which the
heart so deeply craves.

"There lies at the bottom of each man's heart
    A longing and love for the good and pure;
And if but an atom or larger part
    I tell you this shall endure, endure,
    After this world has gone to decay;
    After the universe passes away

The longer I live and the more I see
    Of the struggle of souls towards the heights above,
The more this truth comes home to me
    That the universe rests on the shoulders of Love:
A love so limitless, deep and broad
    That men have renamed it and called it Love.
                            —Ella Wheeler Wilcox.

CHAPTER XIV.

SHIP WORK.

"Ah! my jolly tar, here you are in port again. God bless you. See to your helm and you will see a fairer port by and by. Hark! don't you hear the bells of Heaven over the sea?"

—Father Taylor.

AMONG the important services rendered by Mr. Fletcher to the seamen visiting Portland was the procuring the passage of a law by the legislature of Oregon to guard them from that system of land-piracy known as "sailor snatching," or the enticing of the sailors from vessels and harboring them, and then, in any way possible, making merchandise of them for the profit of the pirate. Its provisions were stringent, and the penalty of its violation was both fine and imprisonment. This was a law greatly needed, as many seamen fell under the wiles of these most infamous wretches, and were led to become faithless to their

own honor and to the interests of those in whose
service they were. While he was laboring for the
spiritual and social uplift of these men of the sea,
there was no danger that so observant and
thoughtful a friend would fail to note the advantage of having a shield of law spread between the
sailor and his enemy and destroyer. Up to the
winter of 1888 and 1889 he had been practically
the prey of these spoilers. Now the despoiler himself was put under bonds to let the sailor alone.
The results of this enactment were exceedingly
beneficial, and it was obvious that the work of
spiritual and intellectual culture so earnestly
sought by Mr. Fletcher and the society whose
agent he was, could be much more promisingly
prosecuted than before. This bill, and Mr. Fletcher's agency in procuring its passage, were very
highly commended by the American Seaman's
Friend Society, through its general secretary, Rev.
W. C. Stitt.

The evangelist, in the crowded congregation,
amid the exciting accessories of music and song,
of prayer and appeal, or even the popular preacher
in the ordinary pulpit of the city, would be likely
to account the daily and constant plod of Mr.

Fletcher among the careless sailor-boys aship and ashore, dull and profitless work. It was little seen, not much heard of, but it is very doubtful if any pastor in the city or any evangelist in the churches brought, year by year, so many individual souls to Christ as did Mr. Fletcher during the years we have traced his history. And after all, it is these individual souls that finally make up the aggregate of the great power and life of the church of God. A single grain of sand cannot shore a sea, but no sea can be shored without the single grains of sand. A single atom of granite cannot make a great mountain, but no great mountain can be lifted towards the sky without the atom of granite. One converted man cannot make a great church, but no great church can be made without the converted man. The trumpet's blare, the cymbals clang, the preacher's rhetoric, the evangelist's appeals, the singer's chorus, all and each, are of themselves nothing, and they often blare and clang and shout into the wind for naught. But when a man like Mr. Fletcher sits down beside a sailor-boy and with the strong tug of his loving heart draws that sailor-boy's heart to Christ, and invites him with a consciousness of his own redeemed manhood, and

puts him among God's children and Christ's followers, something real is done; a soul is saved from
death, a new power for good is loosened in the
world of religious dynamics.

Over and over this fact appears to us as we read
the story of his daily work.   See:—

"March 3, 1889. Visited the ship Hornsby Castle, over at
the Albina docks, and took a fine lot of reading to both
officers and men, and also invited them to come to church
to-morrow. I also visited the bark Gartmore, which leaves
for Astoria to-morrow morning at five o'clock, and bade
Mrs. Richey, the wife of the captain, good-bye. I also bade
the boys good-bye. Some of those dear boys have attended
church and prayer meeting with me at Grace Church
while here in Portland. I always like to keep the run of
these dear boys.

March 31. Sabbath morning I visited one ship and talked
with the officers and boys, and gave them reading matter
and invited them to church. After attending to my ship-
visiting I attended Dr. Dickson's class at 1 A. M. and enjoyed a most precious season in prayer and testimony.
This was my old nine o'clock class in the years gone by. I
met some of my old classmates that used to meet with me
then. I used to have conversions in my morning class. O
how many of these dear sailor boys I used to gather in
with me in the class on Sunday morning, and persuade
them to give their hearts to Jesus; and I can say, to the
praise of God, that not a few of them went out of that
classroom "new creatures in Jesus Christ." Why canno·

such results continue if we make such efforts to secure them? The Lord hasten the day when we shall see them again!"

Yes; five hundred people in the great audience room, an eloquent oration in the lofty pulpit, grand music in the orchestra; and in an hour the pleasing entertainment over! Down, or up, in a little room, a consecrated leader, bowing with some penitent hearts at the mercy seat, teaching some inquiring souls the straight way to God, and in an hour leading them out into that light that never was seen on sea or land, and yet is the Light of Life! What a difference. Where is the hiding of God's power? In that little room, with that little band. "There is joy in heaven over one sinner that repenteth."

One peculiarity of Mr. Fletcher's work, as indicated in his daily record, was the promptness with which he always attended to it. Scarcely had a ship dropped her anchors in the river, or tied up to her dock before he was on her deck. Careful, gentle, never obtrusive, he was apt at hand to render any good service and helpful assistance to officers or men. Before the pirates of the shore had reached them he had pre-empted their attention, and often won their hearts.   He shows how careful and observant he was in this regard in the following:—

May 8.   Visited the bark Earl Dunraven this morning, which has just arrived at the Albina docks.   Had an interesting talk with officers and men and invited them to our meetings at Grace Church while they remained in port. There is this peculiarity about sailors: if I can get them to attend service on arrival they will attend regularly while in port.   They are not very particular as to what church they attend, but whichever they go to first they will make their church home while they remain.   I got a good many of them to go to Grace Church, although it is so far up town, and quite away from their latitude."

Passing on May 12th, the 29th anniversary of his conversion, Mr. Fletcher makes most grateful mention of it.   For nearly a generation he has lived and wrought and talked for God and humanity. From a careless rover of the seas he had become a stable citizen of the "Land of the free and the home of the brave."   From a prodigal wasting his substance in riotous living he had become the owner of a good home and a fair competence of the wealth of the world.   He had found a home in the hearts of a great multitude of people that he had led to Christ in the city where he dwelt.   By his unwavering fidelity to duty, and his constantly improving intellectual and spiritual capability, he had secured to himself the friendship and trust of the good people of all denominations. He had broken the alabaster box of precious ointment over so many hearts and lives that the perfume of his good deeds filled all the world much more literally than would be true of the vast majority of Christian men. Surely he well might monument with praise and song the day on whose decision all this blessedness and all this success in life turned. Not only thus, but it were but natural that he should make it a day of new consecration; of a higher uplook and a wider outlook for his future life. This he did, and moved out into that future life with the spirit and mien of a conqueror. He did this, not by becoming exalted above the work he had been doing, but by consecrating himself more completely, if possible, to it. So he says:—

"Sabbath morning, May 26, Visited the bark Assaye, Captain Ritchie. He is a Christian captain. I distributed a choice selection of reading matter, both forward and aft, and spent a most profitable time with both officers and men in trying to persuade them to become sailors for Jesus, and not to remain in the Devil's service any longer. I find on nearly every ship more or less Christian sailors.

especially this last year. Captain Ritchie, who was raised a Presbyterian, told me how much he enjoyed the services at Taylor Street Church, and that that is to be his church while in port. I took him to the city park and from there to my home for lunch, and then to visit the new High School and other places, which he was greatly delighted with."

Not long after the last date there occurred one of those incidents that open to one's view the sad vistas of so many lives. Mr. N. L——, a respected and quite prominent resident of Salem, Oregon, called on Mr. Fletcher to make inquiries concerning his son, W. L——, who had run away from home, and the father had heard that he had gone to sea on the Otterpool, from Astoria. The boy was a good scholar, and the father and family had denied themselves of many of even the necessaries of life to educate him. He could get sixty dollars per month in Salem. Loved and cherished at home, educated through the self-denial of his family so that he could be useful and honorable in the world, he had fallen into the ruinous ways of immoral youth and men about him, and had cast all his own prospects and all his family's trust and hope to the winds and gone off, spurning a mother's prayers and a father's benedictions. The father besought Mr. Fletcher's help to find some trace of his lost boy. The ship Otterpool had sailed for Londonderry, and Mr. Fletcher could do no more than write to the captain at his home port. How many changes and chances are against the future of all such young men. How few of them ever "recover themselves out of the snare of the devil."

On the first day of August Mr. Fletcher writes:

"Visited the ship Scottish Glens at the Albina docks and had a long and profitable talk with Captain Whiteford. He is an Irishman and a Roman Catholic. He asked me if I did not belong to the Catholic Church. I told him I was brought up in it, and then I told him some of my experiences as a Methodist. I told him after I left my ship in San Francisco how I went to the mines, and through the influence of a Cornish miner, who was a Wesleyan local preacher, I gave my heart to God and became a Christian man. My experience, I trust, did him good. I left him in a good humor, and he earnestly invited me to make him another visit before he left port. He said that he always read all the magazines and papers that I brought him, and was very glad to get them.

"August 15. I have written a long letter to Captain Morris Evans, of the ship Otterpool, to Londonderry, Ireland, in regard to the young man mentioned before. Mr. L.—— desires to use my influence with Captain Evans to have the young man return home as soon as possible.

"September 1st, Sabbath morning. Visited the ship Cambrian Queen. Had a close conversation with Captain Thomas, and invited him to Taylor Street Church to hear Bishop Bowman preach; also his officers and men. Some of them went with me, and more came a little later. The Bishop preached a most soul-refreshing sermon from "Blessed is the man that walketh not in the counsel of the ungodly, nor standeth in the way of sinners, nor sitteth in the seat of the scornful. But his delight is in the law of the Lord and in His law doth he meditate day and night." The church was crowded, and hundreds had to be turned away for want of room.

"September 2. Attended the services of the Oregon Conference to-day and heard Dr. H. K. Hines give one of the most impressive addresses I ever heard on the floor of an annual conference, in behalf of a theological school to be established in connection with the Willamette University. The conference closed after a most pleasant session. May the blessed Holy Ghost go with all these dear men of God and give them great efficiency and power during the conference year.

"September 3. I settled up my bank account and left on deposit one thousand dollars at five per cent. per annum. I have got to the place now in my financial matters that I have been working ahead for for some years. My Heavenly Father has greatly blessed me in my work and in my health, so that I have been able by strict economy to lay this amount by, so that, in God's good providence myself nor wife should be disabled by sickness we should have this to fall back upon, and not be dependent on any one. It is all the Lord's, and shall be used as He shall direct."

This is a statement that has in it more than a mere financial exhibit. This young, careless sail or, whose entire earnings while he followed the sea were absorbed by the usual course of evil habits and evil companionship that keep so many by sea and land in destitution and almost beggary; this miner still following the same improvident course, had been lifted by religion out of all these habits that so sadly despoiled him, and put upon a career of industry and economy, and, not only so, upon one of very wide usefulness, and now, just as age was beginning to gray his temples had made him to possess a fair competency of the good of this world. It was, as he so often says, all of God through the faithful service he had given his Heavenly Father. It was a vindication of God's promise, made of old, but made for all time, "them that honor me I will honor; but they that despise me shall be lightly esteemed."

CHAPTER XV.

WIDENING WORK.

"Surpassing grateful for this friendly light,
I haste to raise it to a flame more bright;
    And lo! it grows
Beneath my fostering care until its ray
Illumines far and wide the treacherous way,
    Nor limit knows."

              —La Tourette.

THE autumn of 1889 brought a large increase of the merchant fleet to the port of Portland, and consequently added largely to the labors and responsibility of Mr. Fletcher. With the captains and crews of the vessels that had been annual visitors for years he had formed a pleasant and useful acquaintance, and that acquaintance had been the means of making his character and work well known to many whom he had never seen, and they were thus prepared to receive him with respect and attention on their arrival. It is to be noted, too, in the course of his journal that there were many more Christian officers and men of the vessels than there had been in former years. Large numbers of these had been converted in this port, and mainly under his influence and direction, and to them it was a kind of home-coming, and they greeted Portland as their spiritual birth-place, and Mr. Fletcher as their spiritual father. The relations between himself and his spiritual children grew more and more tender and confiding, and his influence over them more and more helpful. His ceaseless, unwearied attention to them, the kindly hospitality of his home, the soft and tender tones of his voice while his eyes would glisten with the tear of sympathy and solicitude, drew them near to him, and held them with silken cords to his heart. One of the most familiar sights on the streets of Portland was "Father Fletcher," as he was now beginning to be called, in the midst of a company of his "sailor-lads," conversing with them with animated and victorious countenance, guiding them away from the traps and pitfalls that were set on every side for their unwary feet, and leading them towards the safe harbor of the Bethel or the Church. "Jack" was his love, and helping and saving him was the inspiration of his life.

During the month of September he visited at
least two ships a day, conversing with officers and
men, distributing reading and looking most carefully after their spiritual and temporal interests;
entertained many of them at his own home, introduced them to the churches, and thus put a bright
spot into the life of these boys and men that would
be an influence for help to them ever thereafter.
On the 6th of September he writes:—

"I visited five ships and had two of the apprentice boys
of the Cambrian Queen spend the evening with us at our
home. On going to their ship my wife gave them a large
basket of prunes to take on board with them, so that all
hands might have a good 'blow out' with them. These
dear boys always like to come and spend an evening with
us at our home. They receive so little kindness either on
sea or shore that they greatly appreciate that that we are
able to extend to them while here.

"Met Captain Frazier and his wife on shore. They attend Taylor Street Church when in this port, and the Captain always has services on board his ship at sea.

"On the 10th I visited four ships, and found that Mr.
Elliot and Mr. Dodson, first and second officers of the
bark 'Star of Denmark,' and four of the boys went to Taylor Street Church Sunday night. They are Wesleyan Meth-
odists belonging to Belfast. Ireland. as does their ship.

"October 10th. I had two of the bark Nagpore boys,
three of the bark British Army boys, and Mr. Gunn, the

carpenter, to spend the evening with us at our home. After some time spent in singing and conversation, wife got the boys some nice refreshments, which they greatly enjoyed, after which I read a chapter of Scripture and we had a season of prayer, and about ten o'clock the boys left for their ships, highly pleased with their visit, and promising to come again before they sailed for home. I receive many letters from the parents of these boys thanking us for our kindness to them. It makes us happy to be thus remembered by those we have tried to 'serve in the Lord.'

"October 30, Sabbath. I visited the ship Kooringa and had a profitable conversation with the boys and men. I had thirteen of them with me at church at one night service. I was greatly put out with our pastor. I had asked him several times to remember my 'sailor-boys,' as well as my brethren of the sea in his public prayers, but he, like thousands of others, seems to think that poor Jack may look out for himself. There is no class of men that deserves more sympathy and help from the church than sailors, and none that are more bold and steadfast in confessing Jesus than they. Once get 'Jack' converted and he will stand right up and show his colors in any port.

"November 2. We buried to-day James Henderson, aged 40 years, of London, England. He leaves a wife and two children. He was carpenter of the ship Hermione. He died while I had hold of his hand talking with him. I hope the dear man was saved.

"October 13. I had a long talk with some of the boys and men of the ship 'General Pilton,' which was burned off Cape Horn with a cargo of coal on board, bound for the west coast. The crew had a very narrow escape, for, just

as the fire was breaking through the hatches, the ship
'Glen McPherson' hove in sight, and took all hands off.
When the last boat left the burning ship she was one sheet
of flame. The 'Glen McPherson' brought all the officers and
crew to Portland. There were twenty-two of them on
board.

"November 17. Sabbath morning I visited the bark Glen-
effice, left reading matter and invited the boys to church.
Visited the hospital in the afternoon, and read for Brother
Roe the experience of Bishop Foss in his sickness, some
years ago. I also read for him the 14th chapter of John
and had a precious season of prayer with him. We had a
large turnout of the sailor-boys at the services at Grace
Church at night. It was a good day for my soul. Praise
the Lord!

"November 28. Thanksgiving Day. It has been a very
happy day to me. I was able to get 26 of my young sailor
lads to attend the dinner at the Y. M. C. A. rooms. They
compared very favorably with any other 26 lads that were
there. They were well behaved and did credit to themselves.

"December 1st. Visited the ship Eskdale, Captain Mur-
dock. He was here six years ago in the Eskdale, as was
also his second officer, who was then an apprentice in her.
I had a long talk with the officers and men, and invited
them to Grace Church for the night service. We had two
from the 'Clan McPherson,' two from the 'Ben Nevis,' four
from the 'General Gordon,' and two from the 'Crown of
England.' I am thankful to God for the favor He gives me
with these dear boys.

"December 4. Visited four ships, and met with one of

the apprentice boys who was here in the bark Archer six
years ago. He is now second mate of the ship Clemione.
He is a fine young fellow, and above all he is a lover of
our Lord Jesus Christ. That is the reason he has forged
ahead so, and I would not wonder to see him master of
some fine ship in a short time.

"December 6. Visited 8 ships and bid the boys of the
ship 'Crown of England' good-bye, as they are going away
in the morning for England. Myself and wife have enjoyed
many precious visits from these dear boys during their stay
in port. One young lad is the son of an Episcopal Bishop
of Cloyne, Ireland. I know well where it is. He told me
that three years ago he was in Nenagh, within two miles of
where I was born, and we talked of many places I used to
see when I was a little barefoot boy before I ran away
from home to go to sea. How thankful I am to God that
His kind providence has been over me, and that now, in
my declining years He has placed me here to look after
these dear boys and keep them from falling into the hands
of wicked men while in port. Another one of the boys is
the son of Rev. Mr. Morris, an Episcopal minister at Mil-
ford Haven, Pembrokeshire, and I am to write to his father about his far away boy."

In this way Mr. Fletcher closed up the year
1889. His work among the seamen had never
been more blest, and he was realizing more and
more the results of his earlier and more difficult
labors among them. Much of the seed that he
had so industriously and prayerfully cast into the

hearts of his "dear lads of the sea," years ago had sprung up and grown into a ripened harvest, and he was permitted to see it "after many days." The increase of the number of Christian officers and sailors visiting the port was very gratifying to him, and the more especially as he was enabled to connect so many of them with his own efforts in bringing them to Christ. Connected with this was the completion of an enterprise in which his heart had been deeply interested and to which he had contributed to the amount of several hundred dollars in money, namely, the completion and dedication of Grace Methodist Episcopal Church, in the city of Portland. His record of the services on the occasion shows how intensely he rejoiced, especially under the influence of the sermon of Rev. G. W. Izer, D. D., in the evening of the day. No doubt a large part of his joy arose from the fact that Grace Church, while in their small chapel, had been very hospitable to his "sailor-boys," welcoming them most pleasantly to the church services, as well for the love all the churches bore to "Father Fletcher," as for the good they could do to sailors themselves. This interest always continued, even after the society was housed in its new and beautiful house. "Jack" was always welcome to this beautiful church home. Illustrating the results of his work in this regard, we quote from his journal of February 9, 1890:

"Sabbath morning I visited the ship Patterdale and spent a pleasant hour with Captain Tupham and his officers and men and boys. The captain and some of his boys came with me to Grace Church, and also Captain Steel and his wife and two children, of the bark Lorton, with some of his boys; and at night we had Captain Tupham and eight or ten from other ships. I praise the blessed Holy Spirit who gives me so much favor in the eyes of these, my shipmates and brethren of the sea.

February 12th. I got Captain Tupham to come with me to prayer meeting at Grace Church, and he enjoyed it very much, and gave us a good exhortation. He is a good Christian man and holds services every Sabbath on his ship at sea, when the weather permits."

About this time a change was made in the chaplaincy of the Seaman's Bethel, Chaplain Gilpin being relieved and ordered back to England. His personal peculiarities had greatly retarded the Bethel work since his appointment, and, in fact, the success of Mr. Fletcher in his ship work and among the longshoremen was all that prevented a complete failure of the work for seamen in the port of Portland for all the time that Mr. Gilpin had occupied the post of chaplain. Even Mr. Fletcher's work was not nearly as successful as it would have been had such a chaplain occupied the Bethel as would have secured the confidence of the seamen and the respect of the general public. As it was he had to overcome the prejudice the men and officers felt against the chaplain before he could greatly influence them for good. A man of less excellent character and less tender and sympathizing nature than Mr. Fletcher would have failed utterly where he succeeded in accomplishing so much. The method and spirit of his work are shown in the following extracts from his annual report to the Seaman's Bethel Society, rendered in May, 1890:—

"The year has been one of much profit, I trust, in my work. Not having any preaching in our old Bethel or on shipboard by Chaplain Gilpin, I have been enabled to get quite a large number of the officers and apprentice boys to attend services in the different churches. The reason so few sailors from the forecastle are found in our church services is their want of suitable clothing. They will not attend the church services in their shirt sleeves, yet that would not hinder them from attending the Bethel, as they look upon that as their own church. I have made 574 visits to the ships and supplied every ship with a choice package of reading matter, as well as held conversations with many of the officers, sailors and apprentice boys. I have made 67 visits to the hospitals, and attended three funerals of seamen. Twenty-seven apprentice boys and some officers attended with me the Thanksgiving dinner given by the Y. M. C. A., at their hall. * * * I have had four visits from Captains and eleven from officers and forty-one from the apprentice boys at my home to spend social evenings with us; my wife always providing refreshments for them, and we always ending by reading a portion of Scripture and prayer, by which I try to benefit the dear boys that come here in ships. I also keep up a correspondence with many of the officers and boys, and receive many grateful letters from them, which greatly encourage me in my work. I return thanks to the many Christian families in Portland for the abundant supply of excellent reading matter they have given me for my seaman's work. * * * * By the opening of our new Bethel with a new and efficient chaplain, I look forward to the building up of a large society in the north end of our city. I am thankful to God for the favor He has given me with the officers, seamen and apprentice boys while visiting their ships."

This brief summary of the work done by him during the year exhibits only that part of the work that can be counted in numbers. But the greatest good of all his work was in that department that cannot be seen nor counted, in the souls saved and the lives uplifted by his instrumentality.

"This will survive the empire of decay,
When cold in dust his buried heart will lay."

CHAPTER XVI

BETHEL WORK REVIVING.

"Prayer is the tide for which the vessels wait
  Ere they come to Port, and if it be
The tide is low, then how canst thou expect
  The treasure ship to see?"

IN the early part of 1891 a new chaplain, Rev. Richard Hayes, a Presbyterian minister from Fort Wayne, Indiana, arrived to take charge of the Bethel work in Portland, in connection with the Bethany Mission of that church in the north end of the city. This was a matter of great satisfaction to Mr. Fletcher. For a long time, not only had nothing been accomplished in the immediate work of the Bethel, but its influence had been detrimental to the missionary work of Mr. Fletcher. Mr. Hayes had had no experience in seaman's work, but he was a man of good abilities, and a sincere and devoted Christian, and of a kind and gentle spirit, and was well adapted to the work to which he had been assigned. Mr. Fletcher entered heartily into his plans, gave him all the assistance in his power in every way, and thus enabled him to reach the sailors fore and aft readily and efficiently. He made a most excellent impression on the mind of Mr. Fletcher as a man, a minister, and as to his adaptation to the seaman's work. He says of Mr. Hayes: "He makes a fine chaplain, both officers and sailors taking kindly to him." Indeed, Mr. Fletcher, in recording a visit of Chaplain Hayes and his wife at his own home, says that "the chaplain and his wife and daughter, seventeen years of age, are well adapted to the Bethel work. I think he is the best preacher, and the most spiritual one in the city, and the Lord is greatly blessing his work at the 'north end.'"

Within a few weeks after the chaplain's arrival a "ten day's meeting was held at the Bethel. At the first service, of which there was a large attendance, and several arose for prayers. The meeting resulted in a very marked revival, not far from forty being converted, and the entire Bethel work being greatly strengthened. Mr. Fletcher records the conversion of one "fine young Irishman, who was educated a Catholic priest." Mr. Fletcher's own deliverance from Catholicism disposed him always to the most kindly efforts for the deliverance of others, and he greatly rejoiced when one was brought into the conscious "freedom of the sons of God."

Mr. Fletcher's records of ship visitation during the autumn of 1891 show most clearly how very deeply the minds and hearts of his beloved "sailor-boys" had been affected by his work and that of the new chaplain of the Bethel. Some of these records should be given:—

"October 14. We had a most blessed time last night at our prayer meeting at the Bethel. All the boys of the crew of the ship Silver Stream, and five of them go home in her as Christian men, and four others asked our prayers. Visited the bark Cumbrian, Captain Lorton. Found him to be a Christian man. We had nine of his crew and five of Blythwood's crew at our Bethel service at night.

"November 1st. This has been one of our best Sabbaths at the Bethel. We had fine congregations both morning and evening. We had three captains and a good many of our sailors in attendance. Our chaplain always gives an invitation to all who want to seek salvation to manifest it by rising to their feet at the close of our services. Four young men arose for prayers, and in our after-meeting came forward to the altar and three of them gave their hearts to Jesus, and the other one I hope is not far from the kingdom.

"Fourth. Visited the four masted ship Principality. Captain Jones, and met one of my boys that was here two years ago in the ship Enersdale, as an apprentice. He is now second mate of this fine ship. I am so glad to see so many of my dear boys 'forging ahead,' and looking to become masters. May the Lord bless them."

The influences of the life and example of Mr. Fletcher upon the ambition of these young sailor boys, and the constant and affectionate attention that he and his wife gave them while in port, assiduously endeavoring to lead them to an earnest Christian life, accounts largely for the splendid progress so many of them made in their profession. Those of them who became Christians at once gained a standing with those who employed them, and if they had the intelligence for higher service they were sure soon to rise to it. A sailor is not necessarily able to take command of a ship because he is a Christian; but a Christian young sailor is far more likely to soon become able to do so than one who is not. He is more studious and steady, has a sense of duty that the other has not, wins the confidence of his employers by his trustworthiness, and soon finds himself well up towards the respon-

sibility and opportunity of command, while the
others grope and tug before the mast from year to
year until all aspiration dies out of the heart, and
they give up the struggle of life to what they call
"fate," but which is really only folly. The one
thing that made the uneducated and careless sailor
boy, "Bill Fletcher," the esteemed and honored
citizen, the earnest and successful "seaman's missionary" for more than forty years in one of the
great ports of America, made many of these "cabin boys" and "forecastle lads" officers and commanders of great ships, and that one thing was Religion; the love of Christ and the service of God.

"November 29. This has been another good day in our
Bethel services. At the night service we had a large congregation, and at the after-meeting six came to the altar
for prayers, four of whom were my sailor-boys. Three of
them gave their hearts to Jesus, and have taken Him as the
great 'Captain of their Salvation,' for the remainder of
their voyage of life. I told them that with Christ in the
vessel they could smile at the storm.

"January 3, 1892. Sabbath morning. Visited the ship
Kirkcudbrightshire, Captain Purdy. He has his wife and
child on board with him. I left them reading and picture
cards, and invited them to our services, then went forward
and spoke to the men and had a good time with them, and
got several of them to go to the services with me. As this

is the week of prayer we will hold services every night.
We had one of the best congregations to-night that I have
ever seen at our Bethel. Fully forty of our sailors were
with us in our after-meeting. Twenty came to the altar
for prayer, among whom were ten of our sailors. How my
heart leaped for joy as I bowed with them in prayer to
God, and before the meeting closed to hear from their own
lips that Jesus had pardoned their sins and they had taken
Him as their companion and friend for the remainder of
the voyage of life."

This character of work continued steadily day
after day, week after week, and month after month;
illustrating the peculiar tenacity and fixedness of
the character of Mr. Fletcher. "His heart was
fixed, trusting in the Lord." Whether others were
faithful or faithless, earnest or negligent, he never
faltered nor turned back. His heart was ever going forth in quest of his oft-mentioned "brethren
of the sea," and his steps were never so light as
when he was piloting them to the house of the
Lord, or guiding them to a resting place in the
shadow of the sanctuary of God.

In July, 1892, he was granted, in the kind providence of God, an unspeakable satisfaction in meeting the devoted Christian woman, who, thirty-two
years before, was the instrument of guiding his dark

and ignorant soul to the Saviour in the wild mountains of California, and whom he had not seen for
nearly thirty years, Mrs. Renny, whose name the
reader will recollect in the early part of this narrative. Herself and husband, passing through the
city, took pains to seek out their old mining friend,
and for a few hours there was such an interchange
of heart as does not often come in the lives of wandering mortals. Old hours were new again; old
but not forgotten loves were rekindled, old songs
were sung, and with a newer, sweeter life, both
went on their way to the final reunion where there
will be no separation. It will come at last.

"There union shall be sweet,
At the dear Redeemer's feet,
When they meet to part no more,
Who have loved."

The closing up of this year in the work of the
Bethel with which Mr. Fletcher's ship work was so
closely identified, showed it to have been a year of
signal prosperity. The annual meeting of the
Bethel Society occurred in March, and the reports
of Chaplain Hayes and Missionary Fletcher showed
that more than 1200 seamen had attended the services, and over 100 sailors had been converted in the

meetings. The reports throughout were of the most encouraging character. Mr. Hayes makes special mention of the labors of Mr. Fletcher, "who has performed his duties, not of labor, but of love, faithfully and well." It had been a very happy year to Mr. Fletcher. The change in the chaplaincy had brought spirituality and life, where there had been formality and death. It was no longer necessary for him to try to get his "sailor-lads" from the forecastle to the cushioned pew of the fine church among a fashionable congregation in order to bring them under the influence of a gospel that would save. They were far more ready to go to their own church, the Bethel, where they felt much more at home, and where, during the past year, they were sure to have a pure gospel interestingly and lovingly preached, and where a warmhearted chaplain was as ready to speak the kindly word to "Jack" in his shirt-sleeves as he was to address the "gentleman" in broadcloth, and where such kind-faced saints as "Father and Grandma Fletcher" were ever ready to give him the help and hope that only true love can give another. At these Bethel services he reaped the results of his sowing of the seeds on the decks of the ships among "the sailor-lads," and gathered many a sheaf into Christ's garner, the seed for whose growth had been sown in some kind word spoken, some leaflet put in the hand, some smile written on the sailor-boy's heart in the forecastle. His work was helped now, not hindered, by the spirit and work of the chaplain and his family. It was all a joy and delight, and Mr. Fletcher's heart was filled with gratitude and his life with praise.

Sufficient time had now elapsed since Mr. Fletcher began his work among the young seamen and apprentice boys on the ships visiting Portland for him to begin to see the splendid results of that work. Some, of whom we have spoken in our earlier pages as being led by him to the services of the church and the Bethel and there yielding their young hearts to God, are now reappearing in positions of trust and confidence, still steadfast in their Christian faith and abounding in the work of the Lord. Some reference to some of them, indicating the mutual affection existing between them, may profitably be made. Thus he speaks:—

"August 4th. I have written a long letter to Hughie McLean, one of my sailor boys who is now in San Francisco, in his old ship, City of Madras, as her second officer.

Hughie is a fine Christian boy of a good family in England. I expect to see him captain of some large ship yet. How I love to see these dear boys forging ahead. I have seen many of them come here in their ships wicked and godless, and after being with us a few weeks go home in their ships Christian boys. I trust, by my humble efforts in leading them to Christ while here in port.

"September 24. Sabbath morning. Visited the ship City of York. Captain Jones. He is a new captain. She was here on her last voyage and three of our Christian boys are yet on her. I was glad to find them still faithful to Jesus as their Captain, and they were glad to be at our services again. At one night service Mr. Francis Millman, third mate of the ship Vandurara, united with us and will take a letter from us home. We also had another of the boys of the bark Forfarshire converted at our night service. This makes five of her boys that have been converted since she came to Portland this time. This has been the best voyage these boys have ever made, and they will never forget Portland as their spiritual birthplace."

During the remainder of the year 1893, about three months, Mr. Fletcher was very actively engaged in visiting ships, distributing reading matter among the sailors, inviting officers and men to the services at the Bethel, and in every way helping forward the "men of the sea" in the good life. He made not less than a hundred visits to ships, and records the conversion of a large number of sailor-

boys. The year closed most prosperously for the
Bethel work. The year went out on a Sabbath,
and Mr. Fletcher makes this record of its closing
day:—

"Sabbath morning. Visited the bark Annbree, Captain
Steel. I had a good visit with the captain. He visited this
port on his last voyage. He has new officers with him this
time, and only two of his old boys are with him on board.
The morning being stormy, we only had a small turnout at
our service, but at night we had a full house, with a large
number of our officers and seamen. Our chaplain preached
a good, strong sermon from Isaiah i. 18: "Come now, and
let us reason together, saith the Lord; though your sins
be as scarlet, they shall be as white as snow; though they
be red like crimson, they shall be as wool.' At the close at
least thirty arose for prayers, and eternity alone can re-
veal the good that was done. The year is closing up well
with us in our Bethel work. I praise God for the favor He
has given us with our brethren of the sea."

CHAPTER XVII.

SOWING AND REAPING.

"We must be here to work.
And men who work can only work for men,
And, not to work in vain, must comprehend
Humanity, and so, work humanly,
And raise men's bodies still by raising souls.
As God did, first."

Mrs. Browning.

THE whole course of this narrative illustrates how clearly Mr. Fletcher comprehended the motives and purposes of the average man, and how skillfully he was able to appeal to him for his good. He worked humanly and yet with a divine intent. Always watching for an opportunity to do more good, he was never obtrusive in his approaches. When on shipboard he never, in the slightest degree, interfered with the men when they were employed. The officers soon learned that not only did his presence not interfere with the attention that the sailors were expected to give

to their duties, but that his example of precision
and care was a real benefit to them.   Many officers
who paid little or no attention personally to his
teaching soon learned to welcome his coming
among the sailors because they were the more attentive and tractable for his presence.   This was
the highest possible testimony to his worth, as, in
fact, it was to the things he taught.   His own life,
through the very reaction of his faith on himself,
was rounding constantly into a more complete and
symmetrical fulness, and all men "took knowledge
of him that he had been with Jesus."   He did not
depend on his own eloquence of speech, nor on any
power of personal appeal, nor yet on any worldly
influence that he could command to dispose men to
enter a new life, but he tried simply to introduce
them to Christ, and then trusted to the power of
the Divine Spirit to make his instrumentality sav-
ingly effective in their salvation.   His success in
his simple methods was often marvelous, so that he
was really a divinely accredited evangelist without
any of the professional evangelist's conceit and pre-
tense.   He wrote his name not so much on the
pages of the public prints as on the living hearts
of the men he so earnestly and lovingly sought to

bring to Christ. He could not but be conscious
of his influence over the men of the sea, but it did
not exalt him, though it kindled the deepest gratitude in his heart. As the years wore on, and the
number of those converted by his instrumentality
multiplied, his home in Portland became more and
more a Mecca to sailors, officers and masters of
ships from all over the seas, and in it Mr. Fletcher
and his wife dispensed to them all a simple, charming hospitality, that was always sanctified by the
presence and Spirit of Him who stilled the waves
and hushed the storms of Gallilee, and they looked
with an ever increasing affection on the man who
had led them to the peace which His presence im-
parts. Masters of ships, whom, as wild, wayward
sailor boys, he had led to Christ, and then watched
over tenderly while in port, following them with
letters after they had gone away over the seas filled
with counsel and encouragement, came back again
to crown his aging brow with the garlands of their
gratitude and bless his ever-young heart with their
benedictions.

In the report of the work of the Bethel for 1894
occurs this significant sentence: "The number of
vessels in port has not been as large this year as

last, but one hundred and five have professed faith
in Jesus, and trust in Him above for salvation.   It
has not been an unusual thing to see captain and
officers of the same ship making profession of their
faith and to hear their voices in prayer as they met
with us in the house of the God."   While we do
not claim all this as the result of Mr. Fletcher's labors alone, still for many years he had been the
moral centre around which this great work had
gathered, and without him it could not have been.

Early in the autumn of this year the health of
Mrs. Fletcher began to fail under the influence of
advancing years, and she was compelled to spend
several weeks in the hospital under the care of
trained nurses and skillful physicians.   His care of
her and attention to all her wants was marked by
especial tenderness, and, added to the unrelaxed
calls of his work among his sailor-boys, pressed his
vigorous body and busy mind to their utmost.
Yet no duty was neglected and no call of affection
unheeded.   His strength was as his day, and re-
joicingly he bore his burdens of duty and love onward by the ever-present help of Him who helpeth
man.

Among the many plans for the happiness and improvement of his "sailor-boys," in which Mr. Fletcher took a deep interest was the opening of a "Reading Room" in the Mariner's Home. About the close of November, 1894, it was completed, well furnished with books and periodicals, and ready to be dedicated to its intended use. A large gathering of the pastors and members of the various churches of the city was in attendance, together with many officers and sailors from the ships in port, and with speeches and songs and good cheer it was set apart to its beneficent work. This was a very pleasant and helpful resort for seamen, taking them away from those places for drinking and gambling which always abound in seaport towns, and surrounding them with a refining Christian influence and a pure religious life.

The annual merchant fleet that reached Portland this fall was so large, and Mr. Fletcher's visits to them so numerous that it is impossible to give more than an occasional reference to them. On the 27th of January, 1895, he writes:—

"Visited the ship Carnarvon Bay. I met her owner, who is here on a visit. He is a Welshman, and owns several ships, and is here looking after their interests. He is a good Christian man, and told me he had just discharged the captain of this ship for drunkenness, and sent him home. He wanted me to look after his boys for him while they were in port. At our night service in the Bethel we had over sixty officers and seamen present. I gave them a fifteen minutes exhortation. The blessed Holy Spirit greatly helped me in urging upon them His service.

"February 20th. Visited six ships at the Albina docks and met some of the boys that were here three years ago. Some of them were converted while here then, and they are still faithful to Jesus as the Captain of their salvation. Out of all the young men and boys that have been converted while here in Portland with us, I have not found one that has backslidden; all have been faithful, and some of them have done good work in the saving of their shipmates on the way home from here. It is a great comfort to me to know that my humble labor for them has not been in vain. So I thank God and take courage."

In this connection it is proper to notice the report of the Rev. W. O. Forbes, who had taken the place of the former successful chaplain, Rev. Mr. Hayes, in which he speaks very approvingly of the work of Mr. Fletcher, relating especially to the influence of the Reading Rooms which had come to be called the Seaman's Institute. He says:—

"That the work has been appreciated may be seen not only from the attendance, but from the numerous letters that have been received from seamen after leaving. Here are a few of these testimonials: A chief officer says: 'I am only sorry I did not go to the institute sooner. It seems now more like leaving home than going home. Be sure the next time I come to Portland the first place I make for will be the mission.' An apprentice writes: 'I have never been in a port where the boys have been so well cared for as in Portland. You have the best place of the kind I have ever seen in any country.' A second officer says: 'I've been in almost every port in the world, and I've never been in a place where so much pains is taken with the seamen as here, and I'm only sorry they don't appreciate it more. A sailor said to me: 'I've been all over the world and in many Institutes, but for Jack this is the best place I've ever been in. Everybody seems to be treated alike here.' And just this morning I received this letter from a chief officer: 'The boys all seemed terribly downhearted in leaving Portland, and I quite believe that the attractiveness in the evenings of your admirably conducted Institute has much to do with it. * * * * You may not meet with all the reward from the sailors you deserve, but when good seed is sown there is always some cast on soil that bears good fruit; and then, above all, there is Christ's reward.' "

This was the beautiful culmination of the self-denying work that Mr. Fletcher had been doing for so many years; much of the time alone, often amidst great discouragements, yet going steadily on sowing the good seed in the early morning and in the late evening, hoping, praying, believing, that God would water it from on high, and in His own good time let him see the bountiful harvest. Surely the workman was receiving his hire. Mr. Fletcher writes, May 7, 1895:—

"I attended the funeral of William Norman Harzeel, an apprentice on the ship Highland Home, a native of Devonshire, England. He was drowned yesterday morning. He was a good Christian boy, converted with several other boys in our Bethel meetings here two years ago. He was at our services last Sabbath, and I had conversed with him just before he left the Bethel to go on board his ship. I little thought then that it was the last conversation I would ever hold with the dear boy.

"September 1st. Our young people connected with our Bethel work have organized a 'Floating Society of Christian Endeavor,' in connection with our seaman's work. I have been trying for some time to get it started, and have succeeded at last. I am sure it will be a great blessing to the young men and boys of the ships. I look for a most blessed work among them this winter.

"September 3d. Visited the fine four masted ship Drumonur, Captain Withois, just arrived from New Castle, Australia. As I was standing on the dock Mr. Sitford, her first officer hailed me. I did not recognize him at first, until he jumped ashore and took me by the hand. I asked him if I did not call him 'Jock' when he was here, an apprentice, some nine years ago on another ship. He said he was the same 'Jock.' He was a good Christian boy when I used to call him 'Jock,' and he is now first officer of a fine ship, and a good Christian man. His captain is a Christian, and more than half of his crew are Christians. They have service every Sunday at sea, both fore and aft. There is no swearing nor vile talking aboard that ship.

"October 2d. Visited the bark Glenafton, Captain Beattie. He is one of the young lads that I used to bring up to spend a social evening with us when he was here some years ago. He had passed out of my recollection, though myself and wife did not pass out of his. He said he had never forgot the many little acts of kindness we had shown him and the other boys when they were with us in port; but what cheered me most was his saying that he had put into practice the counsel I had given him, to give his heart to God and take Christ as his Captain. I find him to-day a fine young Christian captain; one who is respected and loved by his officers and crew. I had a precious visit with him. Praise the Lord."

The reader will see that by this time in the life of Mr. Fletcher there was much of the ripened fruit of the seed he had so long been industriously and prayerfully sowing being brought back to him to his great satisfaction and enjoyment. Boys had grown up to be men since he began his work. The frail little apprentices that he and his good wife looked after so tenderly, whom they fathered and mothered so anxiously while they were in port, and from the door of whose hearts they hunted away the wolf of sin so vigorously and courageously, had passed through the necessary grades of service and

not a few of them walked the quarterdeck digni-
fied and able commanders of the finest ships that
entered the harbor.   Others of them had gone out
from his guiding hand into the even more honorable work of the gospel ministry.   Is it any wonder
that, as Mr. Fletcher passed beyond his three score
years and began to study, in the light of a fulfilled
hope, the results of his work that his heart grew
warm, and praises were continually mounting to his
lips.   Surely to have lived so long and lived so
well, and in that life have wrought so faithfully for
God and so successfully for humanity, were an occasion of triumph that comparatively few ever enjoy.   Then, too, that beautiful ripeness of heart
that is often manifested in people who are nearing
the end of the hard, foot-sore journey of life, and
can already see the open door through which they
are so soon to pass into the life immortal, was clearly seen in him.   And there was yet another fact
that threw over all he did and said and was an odor
and a radiance from the groves and the sunshine of
the Paradise of God.   The wife, who had been to
him so loving a companion, so steadfast a friend,
so courageous a helper, so devoted a mother to his
"dear sailor-boys," was rapidly dropping off the

mortal and just as rapidly putting on the immortal.
Thus he was talking and walking in the very language of Canaan, and under the very verdurous
shades of the groves that margin the river whose
waters make glad the city of God. On Sabbath
morning, January the 17th, 1896, she passed gently
out of his sight, and was at rest with the Lord.

CHAPTER XVIII.

"GRANDMA FLETCHER."

> She was sent forth
> To bring that light which never wintry blast
> Blows out, nor rain nor snow extinguishes—
> The light that shines from loving eyes upon
> Eyes that love back, till they can see no more."
>
> —Landor.

FROM various notices given in the preceeding pages it has been made obvious to the reader that Mr. Fletcher found his most constant and sympathizing helper in the great work he wrought among the seamen, in his wife; well known by nearly every sea-faring man visiting Portland as "Grandma Fletcher." This was with them a term of endearment and respect. She was so true, so constant, so tender, so attentive to her sailor-boys and so constantly caring for their comfort and safety while in port, and prayed so earnestly and lovingly for them when away, awaiting their return with so much solicitude, and welcoming them back

again to her heart and home with such motherly
affection that they could not but bear her image
with them as they sailed all seas and anchored in all
ports. It was not that she was young and beautiful, for she was aged and plain. It was not that
she was brilliant and fascinating in talents and conversation, for she was simple and childlike. Why
was it, then, that the thoughts and remembrances
of that plain, unostentatious woman did more to
influence and fashion hundreds and thousands of
lives towards beauty and goodness all over the
world than almost any of her more favored sisterhood in the city where she dwelt? From quarterdeck to forecastle she was beloved by all alike.
Her friendship was cherished while she was living,
and her memory is revered and honored now that
she is dead. None can tell except that in that frail,
plain body dwelt an angel soul; a soul that walked
so deeply and so constantly in communion with
God and the good world that it became a vital
bond of connection between heaven and earth.
Aching hearts felt the consolation of the land of
rest and comfort through her mediation. The
wandering and wayward felt the draw and tug
of her prayers and counsels at their heart-strings,

even when she was far away. The good and
pure felt the sympathy of a common spirit
in fellowship with her; while the bad sighed for
a new life when they saw the beauty and felt
the fragrant atmosphere of hers breathing over
them. In her, one inhabitant of heaven walked
among the sons and daughters of earth, if not in
silken and jeweled robes, then in "a meek and quiet
spirit," of greater price in God's eyes than rubies
and silver. Never was purer love on earth than
the love wherewith she was loved by her sailor-
boys as they sailed away or floated back to port.

Her church membership was held in Grace
Methodist Episcopal Church; a church whose
membership and congregation have exceptional intelligence and social standing. She held the same
sweet place in their hearts while she lived, and her
memory is cherished with the same tenderness now
that she has departed, as in the minds and hearts
of her sailor-boys. When it was known that
"Grandma Fletcher," as she was lovingly called by
all, had passed out of the back door of the church
militant and entered the "gate beautiful" of the
church triumphant, all hearts thrilled with a tender
sorrow for their "loss," mingled with a sweet joy

for her "gain;" for surely for her to die was gain.

Those who were present at her funeral, and they were many, will ever remember how "on the verge of heaven" seemed the fair temple where they celebrated her immortal crowning that day..Her pastor, Rev. Henry Rasmus, D.D., whose lips know so well how to weave the witchery of loving and eloquent speech, and whose own heart parented the words his lips uttered on the occasion, delivered an address that might well have been the funeral oration of a Confessor of the church of the purer and loftier ages, which may fittingly crown this chapter of tribute to "Grandma Fletcher," but without which the chapter itself would be without a coronet.

"I have fought a good fight, I have finished my course, I have kept the faith; henceforth there is laid up for me a crown of righteousness which the Lord the righteous judge shall give me at that day and not unto me only but unto all them also that love His appearing," II Timothy, 4th chapter, 7th and 8th verses.

There could not possibly be found a more appropriate text than this for the occasion of this morning's sermon. It was the exclamation of triumph fitting the close of a noble Christian life many centuries ago. It has been fittingly applied to many a Christian life since, and it becomes very appropriate at this time, a tribute of respect and affection to the venerable friend whom it has pleased God to remove from our society and exalt into His own more immediate presence.

After a life of probably more than three score years and ten devoted in an eminent degree to the glory of the Saviour and the temporal and spiritual welfare of her fellow creatures, she has gone from the battle to the crowning; from the keeping of the faith to where faith is lost in the divine wonderland of sight. Though gone, she still speaks to us, her friends, her brethren, in an example of Christian piety as pure and beautiful and attractive I think as the church militant in these latter days is wont to exhibit; and now in contemplation of such a life all beautiful with holiness and shining more and more unto the perfect day, what is there in it to attract, to uplift, to inspire? Much that we never would know of unless we pause to look and think and learn.

Who was this plain little woman upon whose memory we place this tribute to-day? I shall answer, first of all, she was a beautiful specimen of what the religion of the Lord Jesus Christ can do for all. Born again in the state of New York, on the Atlantic coast, perfected in love in Oregon on the Pacific coast, she stood a living monument of the amazing grace of our Lord Jesus Christ. I might challenge you to bring from all the ranks of those who have despised the religion of Jesus a single example of one who served his generation as faithfully as she served hers. She was not great as the world counts greatness. She was humble; she belonged to the lowliest of the earth. Her name will never be heard outside of a limited few, but I think God spoke to His angels saying, "Watch over her for

I will teach men through this comparatively obscure life that the religion of my son can make the lowliest life glorious." We can do her memory no greater service than to say that only the grace of God can make a character like hers.

You want a religion that gives a perfectly satisfactory experience? You want a religion that triumphs over the frets and worries of life; you want a divine grace that can meet life just as life is and transform it into a temple of holiness, a song of peace? Then you can have it in the same religion she enjoyed. The transforming, transporting religion of Jesus.

Again, if you were to ask me who she was, I should answer, "A contribution from that type of Christianity called Methodism." If I have the purpose of God aright in the mission of the Methodist Church, it is her privilege to develop what? First of all, to take the spiritually lame, the halt and the blind and make them leap for joy, and after having done that by putting upon them the impress of her peculiar doctrine, send them forth a peculiar people to spread scriptural holiness over the land.

I think when this woman of God went up to the gate of Heaven there was at that gateway a group of that type of redeemed ones to greet her. I might name some of them: Father Noon, and Northrup and Nelson and Moreland. This church remembers them when in years past they were mighty for God in prayer and testimony and daily life and as you think of them and then of a type of Christianity that is recognized only by the spiritual crutches it is compelled to use; by its halting and limping, how are you impressed by the comparison? Which type moves men towards the cross of Jesus Christ? These rugged, robust men of God, or those who are fearful lest they should go too far if they should launch out into the deep sea of God's grace? Oh, for more lives that are out on the mid-sea of God's mercy. Oh, for more of such living examples read and known of all men, whose fragrance you can no more fence in than you can fence in the perfume of a grove of magnolias in full bloom.

Nor would I pass unnoticed the large sympathies that characterized this amiable yet great life. She belonged to that class of Christians who loved the world as Jesus loved it. Coming down upon its level and meeting its conditions in a manner not repelling but inviting; that bends under the burdens of others and sends a thrill through the nerves of the coming race. In a brief biography prepared by Father Fletcher, I find these words concerning her: "Many are the young men she started in the better way by pleading with them on the streets to attend religious services and by every means available get them under the influence of the gospel." I do not know that any more luminous commentary could be given of any life than this: He loved the souls of men. Better have that written upon the tombstone than the most applauding epitaph that wealth or social position or anything merely worldly can chisel. Right glorious is it that we are coming out into the horizon of such a sympathy. Of infinitely more value is one life to whom in a religious way the blossoming orchard is a living censer before the throne; to whom the sky is a gallery and the clouds are pictures done in water colors than a hundred whose religious experience is a barren landscape. May it please God to baptize this church with the gospel of holy sympathy which stretches out its hands after the souls of men.

Then I would not fail to remind you of the simplicity of her faith. It was the charming simplicity of a little child asking for what it had no thought of being denied. To her the religion of Jesus was not an intricate system hard to be understood and difficult to put into practice, but was the simple asking and receiving from the hand of her Heavenly Father. Is not that the lesson we all need to learn in a fuller way than we have yet learned it? When Christ began the world's conquest, what kind of a religion did he offer to men? The plainest that had ever been formulated for humanity. Why did he not go down into Rome where there were plenty of great intellects and there get his disciples? Why did he, instead of these, take men who were as plain as the fishing boats by the Galilean sea? I will tell you why. It was because when his words and religion were to be delivered to the world he did not wish them put into learned sayings and apologetics, but in the plainest phraseology so that the humblest could understand them. The religion of Christ never clouded the mind of any one. It is only man's attempt to enlarge upon it that throws the clouds around its plain simple ruggedness. Here is the whole plan of salvation in a few sentences: Man lost because of sin. Jesus Christ the only Saviour. Simple faith in God, simple faith in His Son, simple faith in the Holy Ghost; the one triune God, blessed and glorious. No need to get lost in that creed. Do you want to know who this infinite God is? No need to speculate about it. Ask Him and He will demonstrate who He is in a way that all human philosophy can never overturn. Are you in the throes of any great difficulty or trouble? Simply ask Him to help you out and do your best, and He will come as certain as God is on the living, eternal throne.

Suppose we were to exercise that simple faith in the Bible instead of a spirit of criticism, what would be the result to our individual lives? There is no book in the world that demands such simplicity of belief as the scriptures and yet nine-tenths of Christian men think it is an enigma, hard to unravel and understand. There is only one way to take this letter from our Father's hand, written in the light of our Father's face. Does it say "He hath loved you with an everlasting love? Believe it? Does it say He has a father's kiss for the prodigal's return? Believe it and get that kiss of welcome as speedily as possible. Does it say He will never leave you nor forsake you? Believe it and go right forward, though it may be into the face of flashing lightning and the angry mutterings of the storm. Just as certain as you begin to question whether His promises are certain or not, you have closed those golden lips and their assurance is hushed to you and they become null and void.

Do you still ask me who this woman was who went out to God last Sabbath morning? I reply, she was a woman of much prayer. Prayer was the chalice in which like Rachael in olden times, she brought the waters from the everlasting well. It was the ladder by which she climbed up to gather the grapes hanging over the walls of heaven. It was the ship that carried away her wants and came back with a return cargo of divine help. This plain little woman found what the philosophers failed to discover, the power that moves the world. Prayer was the lever, the divine promise, the fulcrum and the arm of her faith pressing down on such a lever, she possessed the medium that can move not only the earth but heaven also. This church has no doubt lost in this Mother in Israel who for several years was confined to her home, one of its strongest pillars. Around that pillar was twined the beautiful, the true, the love of prayer as the acanthus leaf around the Corinthian pillar. You may not lack in active, devoted vigorous men and women, but if this church has one intercessor left, one so mighty with God, one who so loved to talk with Christ about blood-bought souls; one such Miriam to hold up the hands that are ready to fall; if so, it will prove a vital church.

This, the spirit of earnest prayer, some of us need most of all. What is the infidelity and moral corruption and world-liness of an entire city over against one faded face, wrinkled with years, uplifted to God in almost continuous supplication? Nothing but a starveling; a retreating foe. No wonder that Havelock went on from victory to victory. If his army was to march at six o'clock, he would rise at four o'clock and spend the two hours upon his knees before the throne. You had better not get in the way of a man or woman who has been looking into the face of Jesus Christ, for they may prove a thunderbolt swung by the arm of the Lord omnipotent.

Then, still further, I cannot avoid the conclusion that the latter years of this saint of God have exhibited one of the most attractive instances it has been my good fortune to notice of a beautiful Christian old age. Her religion was so vital and pervading that it seemed always young, always instinct with the freshness and joyousness of perpetual youth, and her religion stamped its impress upon her whole character, and it seemed to refresh her soul with living waters and make her body a continuous temple of the Holy Ghost. To this established dominion of controling grace I ascribe it, that Mrs. Fletcher was to the day of her death exempted beyond most other aged persons from the weaknesses of old age. She had not the slightest spirit of captiousness, of complaining or discontent. But with all of the saintly love, she was as amiable and meek and gentle as an angel's presence. Hers was indeed a peaceful and glorious sunset not behind clouds, but dipping into the golden sea.

I do not know through which of the twelve gates of heaven she entered when she ascended a week ago, but I think it must have been the most glorious of all. And now as we stand in the presence of these three score years that may seem to us like a little sea, each billow crowned with glory and honor, the reflection comes to us that life is inexplicable except as a probation. Why does man live? Why does he die? Take the answer of the old catechism, "to glorify God and enjoy Him forever." What is the true theory of life; what with all its trials, sufferings, heartaches? This: a place of probation; the first stage of an endless being; the waiting room of eternity, where we stay a little while for instruction and discipline, preparatory to the higher pursuits and enjoyments to which if found worthy we are shortly to be promoted. Three score years and ten constitute a period long enough for the purposes of religion. We note as an historical fact that the foundations of piety are almost always laid in early life, and that very few are converted after 60 or 70 years of age. For all practical purposes the probation of the impenitent sinner has usually closed before extreme age has robbed his limbs and his intellect of their vigor. Continue his life to the probation of Methuselah and it would be useless. It would be heaping up wrath against the day of wrath. If we could see as God sees, how many unwritten epitaphs we might read like this: "Ephriam is joined to his idols. Let him alone."

What is the meaning of every church tower from Portland to New York; from London to St. Petersburg; from Moscow to Rome? They are God's finger boards forever reminding men that just a little farther on the life's probation will close and then not an eternal sleep, not annihilation, not another period of probation, but after that, the judgment. In New England they have what they call a passing bell, tolled whenever one in the village dies. I think I can hear in the ringing of every church bell the warning. "Some one gone from the family, gone from the church, gone from the last opportunity of salvation. Probation ended." With that overmastering thought in my mind, I must ask you to-day, have God's overtures been accepted? Have you settled it? Do you not know that hours once dead can never be resuscitated, that upon all the drops of dew that fall on the grave there will not be one tear of repentance? Better listen to the warning ringing through this old world, ringing for two thousand years; ringing for every man, saying, "How shall we escape if we neglect so great salvation? Now is the day of salvation." And then closely associated with this, comes the other reflection that life after all is only a pilgrimage. Very frequently when her husband would come home from his work among the seamen, he would sit down

and talk to her about the glorified ones with whom she had
been associated in church fellowship in this city. Then her
face would light up with the smile of anticipated meeting
and she would say, "Come along, Grandpa; let's go. What
is the use of waiting?" Life to her, as it is to all of us
who believe in a coming glory, is only a little pilgrimage.
Some of us stop here 20 years, some 40, some 50, some 80.
A few are accommodated in the first-class hotels, more in
the second, the vast majority in the third-rate resorts, but
at the end of the journey it will be all the same a resting
place under the flowers and the clods of the valley. Then
what is immortal of us, if we have been true to God, moves
on and up. If you have any idea that the man or woman
who has fallen asleep in Jesus lies decaying in Riverview
or Lone Fir cemeteries, I have no share in your belief.
They have passed on to a more glorious condition. We
make toilsome journeys to visit beloved relatives and
friends; we gladly cross stormy seas that we may see
magnificent or historical structures or renowned cities or
landscapes or celebrated statutes and paintings, but they
have taken the easier and shorter passage to heaven, where
Jesus in His glory sits at the right hand of God, where are
the glories of immortalized sculpture, worked not in cold
stone, but in the living marble of heaven, where are the
landscapes that never fade, where is the city whose splen-
dor outshines the sun. Why, my friends, you cannot understand fully the difference between life here and life
where light is dimless. More difference than between an
eagle in an iron cage and an eagle pitched from Mt. Hood
toward the sun. They have gone out to be deathless as

God is deathless. Brothers, are you ready to close earth's pilgrimage and go out to such an existence?

But there comes yet one other reflection. I could not help thinking, as I rode down the winding hillside after having put her to rest in Riverview Cemetery, what a glorious day the resurrection will be. When the sea shall give up its dead; when the earthquake shall split the polished granite pillar as well as the plain slab. Those monuments upon which perhaps are but two or three words: "Our Child," "Our Father," "Our Mother," "Our Loved One."

There is the one promise more certain than the eternal hills: "As they have borne the image of the earthly, so shall they also bear the image of the heavenly." They will come up again. The faces that were once dear, that are in our memories now fairer than any lily of the field, shall be ours again. Can you think of anything more beautiful than the return of those from whom we have been parted? I do not care which way the body may fall if God's plow-share shall turn back the soil and give me back my lost treasure again.

The idea of the resurrection gets easier to understand as I listen to the scientific appliances whereby the world is made a whispering gallery. We shall hear the voices that were hushed long ago once more when the eternal morning shall break over the hills, when the voice of Jesus shall say, "Come up. You have slept long enough." when there shall be the flash of rekindled eyes and the joy of the greeting. When following the chariot of Christ up the highway of the sky, we shall look back at the place where we slept so long on the hillside, in the valley under the soughing trees and as they disappear forever, from our lips shall go the

shout, "O death where is thy sting, O grave where is thy
victory." May God give us all a part in the first resurrection.

It will not be amiss to close this brief notice of
the life and influence of "Grandma Fletcher" with
some account of her life before she entered upon
that special work that made her such a notable
power for good in Portland.

Her maiden name was Brown. She was born
in the city of Buffalo, N. Y., in 1821, and was left
an orphan in her childhood, but was taken into a
noble Christian household, that of Mr. Bond, who,
with his wife and three daughters of an exception-
ally pure and lovely character, were devoted members of the old Niagara Street Methodist Episcopal
Church. Here her surroundings were of the
choicest kind. In her fourteenth year she was
converted and became also a member of the same
church, entering at once into all the relations and
opportunities it afforded her for Christian improvement and work. The Bible was her constant companion and study, and much of it was there committed to memory, and gave tone and substance to
her thought all through her life. She was much
loved by the members of Mr. Bond's family, and especially by Miss Grace Bond, who became the wife

of Rev. W. P. Stowe, D.D., for many years agent of the Western Book Concern of the M. E. Church in Cincinnati. In 1861 she removed to California and became a member of the First M. E. Church of Oakland. In 1870 she removed to Portland, Oregon, with Col. Flint and family, and connected herself with the First M. E. Church of that city. Here she became acquainted with Mr. Fletcher, and on the 24th day of May, 1871, they were married by Rev. William Roberts, D. D., then pastor of that church. Not long after this she entered into the experience of "perfect love," and its reality was testified in all her subsequent life and work.

In 1874 the "Woman's Temperance League" was organized, Mrs. Fletcher becoming one of its first members. In all the work of "The Crusade" that followed she was never absent from a meeting, and always answered to her name at roll call for street work. With six other Christian ladies she was arrested and put in jail twice for daring to oppose drunkenness and crime with prayer and song and Christian entreaty. When, on the occasion of her second imprisonment, her husband visited her to ascertain if she needed anything for her comfort in the prison at night, holding his hand and look-

ing tenderly up into his face she said: "No; I
have the presence of Jesus, and that is all I need."

Her experience in the work of the crusade led
her into a wider field of Christian work. Every
Sunday morning she went abroad visiting hotels,
boarding houses and jails distributing tracts and
inviting the people to church, and visiting the poor
and the needy during the week, helping and com-
forting them in every way possible. Only God's
Recording Angel has kept the record of the hearts
she cheered and homes she gladdened during the
many years she threaded the streets, the lanes and
the alleys of Portland, bent on her holy mission.
Soon becoming known everywhere, she was welcomed, as she truly was, a messenger of good to
the high and the lowly alike. Scores were started
by her on a better life. In all her home was open
to those for whom she felt such a motherly solicit-
tude. Sailors from before the mast, officers of
ships, captains and their wives and families, shared
and appreciated alike her hospitality, while the
best Christian homes of the city welcomed her
coming with delight. She often sought the fellowship and sympathy of such devoted and cul-
tured Christian circles as filled the parlors of such

families as the Gills, Northrups, Akins, Connells, Dickinsons, Hills, Hayes, Izers, because her own heart was reinforced by their counsels and prayers for her ceaseless round of duty and toil. Few, indeed, of those whose chances were better than hers, and whose opportunities were much wider than hers, in the city of Portland ever took more steps or did more kindly deeds for the Master and His dear ones than "Grandma Fletcher," and now that she is gone none are more missed in the abodes of want or where aching hearts sigh for comfort, than she.

CHAPTER XIX.

COMING OF THE END.

The tide rolls up, the rippling sunny tide,
    The tossing waves throw diamonds to the sun;
They laugh about the gray old rocks,
    And fill the air with breezy vigor as they run.

The tide rolls out, the clouds hang dark and chill,
    And sadness creeps along the sea and shore;
The dripping rocks stand silent and alone,
    Like silent ghosts of days that are no more.

O life, how sweet thou art when tides flow in!
    When skies are bright and health is in the air,
The sunny waves run o'er the golden sands,
    And radiant hope laughs gaily at despair.

Yet sure as life, there comes the ebbing tide,
    When joy and hope flow backward from the shore,
And dreary wastes, and dull and solemn hours,
    Come in the place of the bright days of yore.

O weary heart, look upward to that shore,
    Where hope is lost in sight that's never dim!
There only is assurance, rest, and peace;
    For there forever does the tide flow in.

           —Sir Henry Taylor, in Toilers of the Deep.

THOSE who followed the unpretentious story of the every-day life of Mr. Fletcher from the time we first introduced him to them must have been impressed with the difference between the man of nearly three score and ten, as he now appears, and the young ignorant Irish boy that he then was. Then he was a thoughtless waif floating on a rough and stormy sea. A score of years afterwards he was but a beaten and buffeted sailor boy, unable to read, given up to ungodliness, without intellectual or moral aspiration, and having no hope in this world or the next. Now he is a well-read man, a close and clear student of religious truth, a well-informed citizen, a devoted member of the church and zealous Christian worker and the friend and associate of the intelligent and wealthy people of the city in which he has resided so long, and his name is a household word among the seamen of every port in Christendom. It is not far nor difficult to find the cause of this great change. One single fact alone explains it. It was his conversion to God, followed by a constant and entire consecration to His service, and the consequent employment of all his powers in doing good to men. The writer does not remember a case in

a fifty years' ministry where a man made his religion more the chief part of himself, and subordin-
ated every fact and interest of his personal life to
God's service as the Holy Spirit revealed it unto
him, than did William S. Fletcher.   It is in this
that his life is a worthy model, and it is in this that
he will yet speak long after "we shall see his face
no more."   It is, therefore, with a feeling that the
tracing out and recording of the facts and incidents
of this life of singular devotion has been a means
of personal grace, and with a conviction that the
record will be a like means of grace to those who
read it, that the writer comes to the concluding
chapter of this volume.

In the middle of the year 1897 Mr. Fletcher records the final conclusion of his mind in regard to
the publication of this memoir while he was yet
alive.   He had expected that it would be published
after his departure, but his best friends desired that
he himself might see it while living, and have the
pleasure of using it personally for the benefit of
his "brothers of the sea," as he concluded his work
among them in his last and ripest days.   This decision made, and all needful arrangements for its
early completion perfected, he decided to fulfill a

long felt desire to revisit some of the scenes of his early life on the Pacific coast, and especially San Francisco, with which he was so familiar when it was but a straggling hamlet of tents and dingy wooden buildings among the sand hills that begirt San Francisco Bay. It was the middle of 1897 when he was ready to take his departure on this long-desired trip, and, in his journal for June 26th, he begins the record of this, a brief pause from the constant toil and care of ship and hospital visitation, and from those other constant demands upon his waning strength that clamor at the door of the heart of all those who are ready to respond to human want by Christ-like help. He says:—

"I leave to-night on the steamer Columbia for San Francisco for a four week's cruise, and I pray that the Lord will keep my little home and all that belongs to me in my absence, and if it is His will that I may be returned again that I may be better prepared for my work in behalf of my brethren of the sea."

Thus first in his mind always was his relations to the men for whom he had spent so many years of tender care and earnest prayers. On his arrival in San Francisco he went directly to the "Sailor's Home," choosing that as his residence while in the city that he might be the nearer those for whom he felt such earnest solicitude. He found great numbers of seamen at the "Home" under the superintendency of Captain Staples, and the "Seaman's Institute" conducted by Mr. Fell, the resort of large numbers of sailors, and speaks approvingly of the influence of them both over the men of the sea. We will let him tell in his own language how he spent his first Sabbath in San Francisco:—

"Sabbath morning, June 20. I attended the morning class at the Central M. E. Church. Had a good class, which I greatly enjoyed. Heard Dr. Dille preach a good sermon, but before its close we had quite a shock of earthquake which caused a big scare in the congregation, and knocked the remainder of the sermon out of the doctor. At night I attended the services at the Mariner's Church, where we had a good sermon by Chaplain Rowell, followed by an after meeting, at which three of the seamen were converted, which brought joy and gladness to their hearts as well as to my own. So ended my first Sabbath in San Francisco.

As this is Jubilee week, there are a large number of sailors ashore from the ships on leave. I meet many who had been to Portland on other voyages. As soon as I was recognized by them I was introduced to their shipmates as "Mr. Fletcher, from Portland, who always looks out for us boys." It seems like home to be among them."

The "seed cast upon the waters" is being gather-

ed now in the gratitude of those to whom he had
been the instrument, in the hand of God, of bringing good in other days. So it is ever. "He that
goeth forth and weepeth, bearing precious seed,
shall doubtless come again with rejoicing bringing
his sheaves with him." Sometimes, it is true, the
time seems to be long, and the harvest may even be
left for others to gather. Mr. Fletcher found
David Jones, a sailor who had often been in Portland, and for whom he had labored most earnestly
in the past, but he found him, as he writes:—

"The same old David, still in his sins. I talked to him
faithfully, and he promised to come to see me and have a
talk with me in my room at the Home, which he did. I
spent three hours with him. I dealt with him faithfully.
I read portions of Scriptures for him, and got him upon
his knees while I prayed for him. I wanted him then and
there to make a clean breast of his sins to God, and take
Jesus as his Captain and Saviour. He was greatly broken
up, but he would not yield to the blessed stirrings of the
Spirit. It was then about half past eleven o'clock, and he
had to leave to catch the last boat to Oakland. He promised me that he would read his Bible and do better."

This incident shows the intense earnestness and
sincere faithfulness of the work of Mr. Fletcher
with his "sailor-boys." With tears in his eyes,

with tenderness in his voice, yet with a faithfulness to truth that is worthy of all praise, he would set before them the "error of their ways" and then, kneeling with them, put their case before God. His prayers were trustful, confidential talks with God. They two were acquainted. They were friends, as God and Abraham were friends. They walked and talked together and trusted each other with a perfect trust.

One of the most refreshing visits made by Mr. Fletcher in San Francisco was with the family of Dr. John Dillon, the son of Rev. Dr. Isaac Dillon, one of his intimate friends and helpers for many years in the city of Portland. He speaks of it with most intense satisfaction, and the more especially as he found Dr. Dillon, whom he had known intimately in his boyhood in Portland, a most worthy Christian man.

The weeks of his stay in San Francisco passed very rapidly and pleasantly. He did not fail to improve all opportunities for good doing, and especially among the sailors wherever he found them. On the evening of the 4th day of July he attended the services at the Seaman's Institute. He makes the following record concerning the services,

which, as it incidentally reveals his own high sense
of religious obligations, as well as indicates his firm
conviction of the nature of the life a seaman's
chaplain should live, we copy:

"I attended the night service at the Seaman's Institute,
as I wanted to see how the Chaplain conducts his work.
There was quite a large number of the sailor lads, besides
several ladies present. I thought it strange to see Mr. F.
through the week playing billiards and smoking and carrying on with the boys, and then to see him don his sur-
plice on Sunday night and read prayers to them. I thought
if this was the way he attempted to win the boys to Jesus
he had greatly mistaken his calling. He might conduct
in this way until doomsday and never win over one boy
to Christ."

With a most genial disposition Mr. Fletcher
could brook no such trifling spirit in one who
sought to "negotiate 'twixt God and man as God's
ambassador," and he never failed in one way or another to put the seal of his disapprobation upon it.
Besides, he rightly judged that a Christianity that
draws no line of distinction between the practices
and pastimes of the Christian and worldly man is a
Christianity in word only, and not in deed and in
truth. No one is quicker than the men that sail

before the mast to detect the counterfeit present-
ment of a Christian life, and no one turns away
from it with a deeper disgust. But the real Christian life wins and holds their confidence, and he
who lives it commands their respect and honor.
Thus it is always and everywhere.

The time he had assigned himself for his visit to
San Francisco having expired on the 12th day of
July, he took passage on the steamer Columbia for
Portland. On his departure he says:—

"Forty-seven years ago I arrived in what is now San Francisco. Then there was no city here. I was then a sinful,
wicked young sailor. When I witness the great changes
that have taken place in the city since then, I feel that
none of them have been so great as that which has taken
place in my poor heart. Glory be to God! Then careless
and wicked, now a child of God, full of faith and of the
Holy Ghost, I cannot find words to express my great love
to my Heavenly Father, to Jesus Christ, my Saviour, and
to the Holy Ghost, my Sanctifier, for their great love to
me."

Surely Mr. Fletcher was right. No material
change can in any wise equal that which transpires
in the soul and life of one "born of a new celestial
birth," "by the power of the word of God which
liveth and abideth forever."

On reaching Portland Mr. Fletcher resumed his work of ship visitation, with the same fidelity and tenderness that had always characterized it. Still he earnestly sought a new spiritual endowment for the work before him. He set apart the hour between six and seven every morning for a special reading of the Scriptures, meditation and prayer that he might be filled with an enlarged faith and increased power in his work. As the autumn came on the largest fleet of merchantmen that had ever visited Portland arrived, and it tasked Mr. Fletcher to the utmost to meet the demands upon his time and means in caring for the spiritual and temporal good of his dear "lads of the sea." The ships were all visited, and not one sailor escaped the attention and advice of this lover of his kind. On the last day of November, 1897, he writes:—

"I have put on board of nineteen ships this month 1273 pieces of reading matter, 206 magazines, 189 picture cards with Scripture texts on them, with a large number of tracts. There has been the largest fleet of ships and steamers in port this season that I have ever seen here, and I look for at last 150 more of them before the season closes."

Early in January, 1898, Mr. D. W. Potter and Mr. E. F. Miller, of Chicago, entered on a season

of evangelistic work in Grace Church, in Portland.
Their coming was hailed with delight by Mr.
Fletcher, and he entered into the work they inau-
gurated with great faith and fervor.   He records
his impressions of the work as follows:—

"I have not seen such a revival in Portland for many
years. It has been a great blessing to Grace Church, and
will result, I think, in fifty accessions to the church. The
meetings were made a great blessing to myself. The
blessed Holy Spirit gave me great liberty in getting a large
number to the altar. He used me particularly in that part
of the work. I had the unspeakable pleasure of seeing
seven of my sailor boys give their hearts to God. I had set
apart about three weeks before the commencement of the
meeting from five to seven o'clock every morning for reading and prayer for the endowment of power for my work,
and I must say to the glory of God that the Holy Spirit did
greatly bless me in my work during the meeting. I also
had a great deal of ship visiting to do during the time of
the meeting, and I trust very many of the men of the sea
were greatly benefitted.

"January 19. I attended the meeting at the Third Presbyterian Church, where all the afternoon meetings were
held. While we were singing as the congregation were coming in, to our great surprise Amanda Smith walked into
the church. As soon as Mr. Potter got his eyes upon her
he cried out: "Why, here is Amanda Smith!" I jumped to
my feet, and sure enough my eyes had seen Amanda
Smith. I had read her book twice over, and read much

about her, but never did I think that I should have the
unspeakable happiness of meeting her in the flesh. O how
my heart was thrilled when I heard her sing and pray and
speak for the blessed Jesus under the power and presence
of the blessed Holy Spirit, as he was manifested in the
words of her testimony. Praise His holy name, such a
meeting was never witnessed before in East Portland.
The result so far of the meeting on the East Side has been
most gratifying from the large numbers that have been
converted at the altar.

"February 5, 1898. Visited the bark Nithsdale, Captain
Steven. I was glad to meet with him and his first officer.
He was here fourteen years ago, as well as on his last voyage. He is a Christian captain and attends Grace Church
when in port. I gave him, and also his boys and men, a
fine lot of reading to take to sea with them. I have put on
board the ships for the month of January 797 papers, 150
magazines, 120 cards, 62 calendars, 7 comfort-bags, 13 new
Testaments, and quite a number of tracts. It has been a
busy month with me in my ship and Bethel work. It appears to me the older I get the more I have to do, but the
Blessed Lord gives me strength according to my duty.
Praise His name."

Thus, as the early months of the present year
passed by, Mr. Fletcher, in the ripened fullness of
grace, continued his loved and consecrated toil.
Confined to his home for some weeks by an accident, he was greatly cheered by the constant attentions of the dear Christian people whom he loved

so tenderly, and who reciprocated all his love, and
especially by a very fraternal communication from
his old comrade and friend in his Bethel and ship
work in Portland, Rev. R. S. Stubbs.   In his re-
sponse to Mr. Stubbs he says:—

"I have been in dry dock for the last few weeks. I have
had a good opportunity to work up my latitude and longi-
tude, and find out my bearings. My dear chaplain, I can
say with you, by taking good heed to my chart and sailing
orders I have no fear of making shipwreck of faith, for I
don't intend to have any dead reckoning to work up at
the end of life's voyage, for I want an 'abundant entrance'
and to be safely moored with our loved ones at last. Praise
the Lord."

Thus for so many years we have traced the
course of the life of this true saint of God from its
unpropitious beginnings in his low-roofed Irish
home through the reckless and untaught career of
a man "before the mast;" through the struggles
and adventures of a miner; in the church, in
plain and earnest Christian toil, until we find him,
as his years touch three score and ten, an honored
Man, a trusted Friend, a consecrated Christian,
waiting only the good call of God to his final glori-
fication.   Not more fittingly did Paul say of him-

self, as he neared the end of his earthly career, than Mr. Fletcher can say as he nears the same goal:—

"I have fought a good fight;
I have finished my course;
I have kept the faith."

FINIS.